FORGING THROUGH UNKNOWNS:
THE SEAGIRLS' ALASKAN ADVENTURE

KB TAYLOR

kb-taylor.com

BOOT TOP BOOKS
Lacey, WA

Library of Congress Cataloging-in-Publication Data
Bishop, Karen (KB Taylor), Illustrations: PB Taylor
LCCN: 2021953392
Forging Through Unknowns:The Seagirls' Alaskan Adventure/KB Taylor-1ˢᵗ ed.
p. cm: includes bibliographical references.
Summary: After Daddy is spotted on a schooner heading to Alaska to dig for gold, twelve-year-old Aggie and her two younger sisters set sail aboard the *Irene* to find him. Upon arrival, they face unknown obstacles: icebergs, angora goats, rugged prospectors, and a treacherous hike up White Pass.
ISBN: 9781733369787 (Paperback)
1. Self-reliance—fiction. 2. Steamboats and machinery—fiction. 3. Klondike Gold Rush (Alaska) 19ᵗʰ century—fiction. 4. Sisters—Fiction.
Printed in the United States of America
Dec 2021
Boot Top Books, Lacey, WA

ACKNOWLEDGMENTS

Thank you to my dad and my grandmother for their love of steam, cherished stories, and enthusiasm for keeping the Cline history alive.

To my sister, Diane, for her creative acuity to review on both sides of the lens: as an editor and a reader.

To my husband, who is my foundation and possesses the distinctive talent for bestowing the best cup of coffee when desperately needed.

To my Aunt Ruth for her continued support and superior proofreading to finalize the story.

To my cousin, Vickie, as the final reviewer and her comprehensive assessments to make the book its very best.

THE *IRENE'S* LOWER DECK

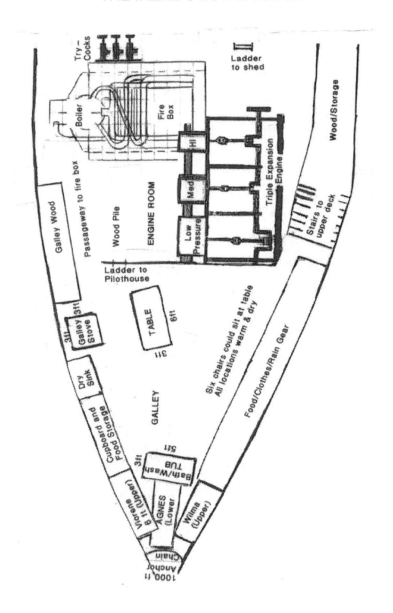

TABLE OF CONTENTS

THE *IRENE'S* UPPER DECK

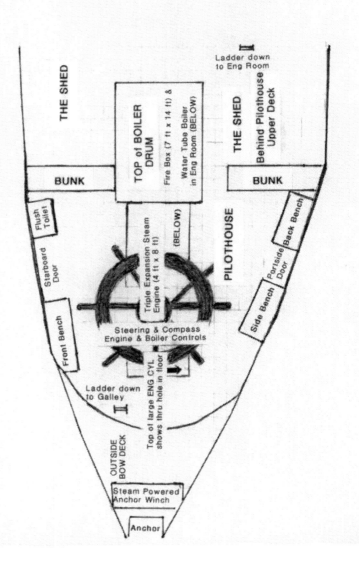

AUTHOR'S NOTE

Steam machinery has been a part of my life since I was a child. My father, Paul Taylor, inherited his love of steam from his grandfather, Fred Cline, and his mother, Agnes Cline Taylor, the inspiration for this book.

My grandmother and her sisters were born in the early 1900's. I pulled the timeline back to incorporate the Alaskan Gold Rush, which my great-grandfather, Fred Cline, experienced. Even though the story is fictional, it's interwoven with facts.

FACTS:

Fred Beckman Cline, my great-grandfather, was born in Oregon in 1874 to German parents. After his father died in a steamboat explosion, Fred was raised by a Prussian family (Kleinsarge). He dropped his surname Beckman and went by Cline. In the book, I used Beckman. During his life, he was a port-light tender, tugboat boiler-man, boat builder, sea captain, fisherman, inventor, and builder of pile-driven fish traps. By 1896, he had learned to build boats, was hired at the Hoquiam shipyard to rig a newly built schooner, and signed on as a seaman on her maiden voyage to Alaska to take miners to the gold fields in Cook Inlet. His story was published in the *Alaska Sportsman Magazine,* in 1954. After he returned from Alaska, he married my great-grandmother.

Mary Belle Cline (Belle), my great-grandmother, was born in 1880 in Rainier, Oregon. Her Portuguese father died when she was two-years-old. After Mary Belle and Fred wedded, they lived in a shack at the mouth of the Humptulips River. For over thirty-five years, she cooked and washed without electricity or plumbing, and tatted over 3,000 feet of netting for the fish traps. The girls also learned this skill.

The Clines had five daughters (no sons). Heather, 1898, lived two weeks, Irene (1902-1904), Agnes— 1903, Viorene—1905, Wilma—1907.

In April 1914, the family sailed the *Irene* to Alaska. Aggie, my grandmother, was eleven. Viorene was ten and Wilma, seven. During this trip, they sailed to Wrangell and were greeted by Presbyterian missionaries. Agnes described the meeting in a 1982 letter: *"Mother had dressed us girls in our best dresses. The lady was Mrs. Frances Clarke. She took us to her home which was the Presbyterian mission. There were flowers blooming in the yard. Mrs. Clarke wrote to me for many years."*

The Clines also anchored in Ketchikan: *"Ketchikan ahead. We could go ashore and did walk the wooden plank streets. We stayed at a long floating dock with other boats. There were rich men's cruisers there too. We bought a few things but everything cost more in Alaska. We did not meet any friends at Ketchikan. We stayed a few days. It began to rain a lot. My schoolbooks of spelling, arithmetic, and reading had been brought from Hoquiam so Mother set me busy if we had to stay in. I was not quite up with the fourth grade class in September, but I finally caught up with the other fourth graders at the Chenois Creek School (Fern Hill)."*

HISTORICAL BASIS FOR THE CHARACTERS:

The *Irene,* built in 1912 by my great-grandfather, Fred Cline, was named for his daughter, Irene, who died at age two.

At sixty feet, the *Irene* was the largest of his nine boats and manned by his three young daughters; one was my grandmother, Aggie.

My great-grandmother, Mary Belle, designed the interior, chose the boat's color—robin's-egg blue—and referred to the *Irene* as her luxury hotel. It had a bathtub and flush toilet, luxuries not found in their wilderness cabin, and a cast-iron stove. It also had a triple-expansion engine and an oversized upright water-tube boiler that could handle four-foot logs on long trips, unusual for this time.

Agnes **Beckman** was based on my grandmother, Agnes Cline—also known as Aggie the Navigator and Captain Paddy. By the age of twelve, she could man the boilers and the triple-expansion engine better than most seafaring men, and she could navigate by the stars. In 1920, the Tacoma Ledger published the article *Captain Paddy—Pride of Harbor.* She was also an artist, discovered her talent in high school, and learned to play piano by ear.

Viorene Beckman was based on my great-aunt, Viorene Cline. My grandmother described Viorene as a sweet-natured girl who liked to read and cook.

Wilmina Beckman was based on my great-aunt, Wilma Cline. She was the only one of the three girls who inherited their mother's Portuguese looks. I was told she loved animals. A photo of her rowing a canoe with a cat inside followed by her pet goose swimming behind supported that fact.

Captain Murphy was based on my father's Danish friend, Holger, a hermit I knew when I was a kid.

FORGING THROUGH UNKNOWNS:
The Seagirls' Alaskan Adventure
(The Seagirls' Adventure Series)

The *IRENE* drawn by Aggie Cline, Age 16 (1920)

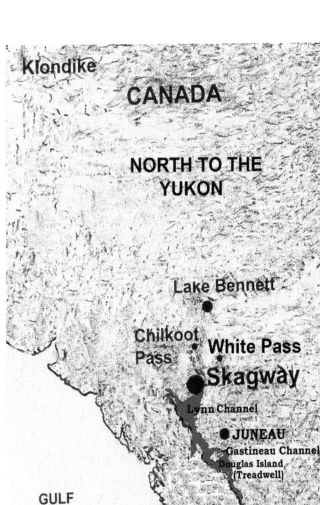

Klondike

CANADA

NORTH TO THE
YUKON

Lake Bennett

Chilkoot
Pass

White Pass

Skagway

Lynn Channel

JUNEAU

Gastineau Channel
Douglas Island
(Treadwell)

GULF
OF
ALASKA

WRANGELL

CHAPTER 1
SOUTHEAST ALASKA
AUGUST 9, 1898

A SOU'WESTER blew across our bow, flapping the edges of our tied-down sails as the sea frothed like a beaten egg. I stood behind the *Irene's* eight-spoke wheel and gripped it tight.

"Never figured Alaska to have such rough waters," I told Captain Murphy, my voice quivering a bit. "It's so much different than sailing along the Washington coast."

"Aye," he said in his Irish brogue while sitting on the front bench with one hand clutched to it and the other to a tin cup splashing out coffee every time a wave sprayed our bow. "Alaskan waters challenge a sailor, that's fer certain, Aggie-girl. But the *Irene's* a strong boat. She can handle it."

At sixty feet, the *Irene* was the finest steamboat Daddy had ever built and powerful as a towing tug.

When the pilothouse bell clanged, I jumped.

"Got to be one of ye sisters ringin' the bell," the captain remarked standing and stepping toward the wheel, his peg leg striking the floor as he approached. "Take a peek below, I'll spell ye."

I knelt down in front of the wheel and looked through a hole in the floor that exposed the engine room beneath. My sisters along with Billy, our thirteen-year-old drifter friend, had been riding below in the galley. When I saw a mess of black hair, I knew it was Wilmina, my eight-year-old sister, who had been pulling the cord. She waved when she saw me.

"Aggie, can I come up? All Viorene wants to do is read, sew something frilly, or worse, give me another good-manners lesson."

Viorene, my middle sister who had just turned eleven, studied every etiquette book she could find and practiced on us at every turn.

"Awful sloppy weather for you to be walking the deck," I said. "Get Billy to play cards or checkers."

She huffed. "He's taking a nap. I'm going to climb up the engine-room ladder."

"No, as rough as it is, you could be thrown off. I'll pull the steam whistle when conditions get better." I went back to the wheel and stood next to the captain.

"Can't blame her," he said. "I'd be jumpin' out of me skin if I got stuck down there."

"Me too," I admitted.

One true benefit as the oldest, I never got confined below. Soon as I turned twelve, Daddy added more teachings about boats. I had already been learning for almost a year, but he said twelve was the perfect age for a girl to sharpen her skills, something to do with my brain now fully formed. But when Mama died three months later, all lessons stopped. Then, Daddy went missing.

"See blue sky pokin' through," the captain said.

Daddy had several *Pacific Coast Pilot* books—a mariners bible of maps, charts, ocean depths, plus other important seafaring facts.

I grabbed the one on Alaska, pushed my blonde hair off my sweaty face, and flipped through the pages I had already marked.

"The blue sky looks to be in the direction to Wrangell," I told the captain. "According to the charts, we should be seeing it soon."

"Wind appears to be movin' toward shore," he added. "Before long, the waves will be flattnin' out."

"Hope you're right," I muttered, closing the book and rejoining him at the helm.

PULLING INTO Wrangell's horseshoe cove, I cupped my hand over my eyes and surveyed rows of shack-like buildings with signage painted on their roofs: laundry, tin shop, dance hall, and saloons, to name a few.

"Wrangell appears to be more civilized than I figured," I told the captain.

"That's good to hear," Viorene said, walking through the pilothouse door with Billy and Wilmina behind her.

"Let's get this boat tied down and do some explorin'," the captain said, motioning Billy and me out to the deck. After we secured the *Irene* to a piling, Billy steadied Viorene off the boat and then helped the captain. Wilmina and I climbed down to the dock on our own.

"Ye girls stay together," the captain said. "Let's meet back at the boat. Might be stoppin' at a saloon."

Knowing the fix the captain's drinking and gambling had caused in the past—forcing a quick getaway in his dilapidated boat, which sank and he injured his leg—concerned me, but I had to let it go.

Captain Murphy was like a grandpa to us, been in our lives from the beginning, and in our search for Daddy, he stepped in to help. I touched the captain's arm. "I'll take you."

"Saloon's not a fit place fer a lass," he said.

But saloons weren't good for Billy either. In the past, he had been forced into a life as a pickpocket. He was now on a path to good, but he sure didn't need to be tempted by the sight of gold.

"I think we should stay together," I added.

"Stop frettin'," the captain told me.

I looked at Billy. Now eating good, he had filled out some. Even his dark hair had lightened to a deep brown, which I attributed to nourishment. However, he was still awful scrawny and if caught stealing by rugged men what a fit that would cause.

With the captain's peg leg slowing him down, my sisters and I got a good distance ahead, but every few steps, I peered over my shoulder, keeping the captain and Billy in my sight. As we neared a saloon, gold-rush prospectors standing outside noticed us.

"You girls get off that floating heap?" a prospector said, then laughed.

Wilmina stopped and glared at the man, but I yanked her along. "Hold your tongue," I told her.

Wilmina, the only one of us with Mama's Portuguese looks, was as daring as a baby raccoon, outspoken too.

We walked on, but got another challenge. This time, it was Viorene who caught the men's attention. Viorene had the temperament of a scared rabbit.

"Ain't you a pretty one," an older prospector told her. He had on tattered clothes and a worn hat, and a scraggly, mud-brown beard covered his chin. "Not many yellow-haired girls in these parts."

Viorene and I both had Mama's lanky build and were blonde and blue-eyed like Daddy. Except her hair was curly and she had Daddy's dimples and perfect smile. I had straight as a yardstick hair and gopher-like front teeth.

Viorene lowered her head and tried to walk on, but he latched onto her arm. Her eyes widened.

"Let go of her," I yelled, pulling on his shirt.

Billy and Captain Murphy must've seen the ruckus, 'cause next thing I knew, they were at our side. "What's goin' on?" Captain Murphy barked. "Unhand her."

"Don't mean no harm," the prospector said, releasing her. "The girl reminded me of my daughter. All dressed up and pretty in her Sunday best."

Holding onto Viorene's arm, the captain escorted her into the general store. "From now on, dress like ye sisters."

I didn't say a word, but I knew he was right. I'd told Viorene she was too dressed up. Wilmina and I usually wore bib overalls and rubber boots. Not Viorene; she was prim and proper in her black cloak, pink gingham dress, black tights, and laced-up boots.

She scowled at me with a heated stare, but I wasn't surprised. We had already traveled as far north as Port Townsend searching for Daddy and debating on what to do next. That is until we spotted Daddy aboard an Alaskan schooner. Viorene voted to sail home to our Humptulips River cabin, but Wilmina and I overruled.

I pulled Viorene with me to the back of the store, out of earshot. Wilmina followed. "Settle down," I told her. "Things are different in these parts."

"Different," she spouted. "These men are uncouth. It's time for us to head for home."

Wilmina shook her head. "Not without Daddy."

I glanced at the captain and was happy to see him in a conversation with the shopkeeper. I turned back to my sisters. "This will all work out. Once we find Daddy, everything will be fine."

Viorene crossed her arms. "We have no idea where he sailed. All we know is his fishing boat was destroyed in a storm and that he might be confused. But he could be anywhere now."

"It's been less than one week when we saw him aboard that Alaskan schooner. He's gotta be in one of these towns."

She threw her hands into the air. "What's the point in saying anything to you?"

The captain hollered. "Girls, come sit."

"Plenty of seats," the shopkeeper added, pointing to six wooden chairs circling a potbellied stove.

Viorene sulked as she plopped down in the end chair, opposite Billy.

"What brings you folks to these parts?" the storekeeper asked, leaning on his counter. "Don't tell me it's the gold."

"No," the captain said. "Searchin' fer a schooner, the *Claudina*. Would've arrived 'bout three days back."

The shopkeeper shook his head. "Don't recall it. Most ships bypass Wrangell and head on up to Skagway."

"How far to Skagway?"

"Depends."

"We have a sixty-foot steamer."

"Two days. Maybe three."

AFTER TWO MORE DAYS in Wrangell, the *Irene* looked like a circus tug: crates, burlap sacks, uneven bales of hay stacked every which way, and crisscrossed clotheslines dangling with pots and pans clanging in the wind as more supplies filled our boat.

This voyage to Alaska was more of a whim than a thought-out plan, but never did I think we'd be tagged as a hauling tub. After Daddy had gone missing, my only mission was to find him.

When I saw Billy maneuvering a cage aboard, I hurried over and looked inside. "Is that a goat?" I asked, staring at the floppy-eared animal with curly locks, spiral horns, and a long hairy beard.

"Yep," Billy replied. "More coming."

Captain Murphy had worked a deal with a man he met in the saloon named Jake. The captain agreed to transport goods in exchange for dry wood.

With the Alaskan rough seas, we had burned through most of our wood supply and quickly discovered that wood was not as easy to retrieve in Alaska as the driftwood along our Washington beaches.

I zigzagged around barrels and boxes to the pilothouse. "Captain," I called out.

He set up and yawned. "What's the panic?"

"They stopped loading our wood at half, since the *Irene* is packed from stem to stern. Did you know they were bringing goats?"

"No," he said, grabbing my arm and steadying to his feet. I quickly followed him out the door as he headed to a tall man who was standing next to Billy.

"Better not be playin' me," the captain hollered. "This is twice what ye advertised. And who authorized goats?"

Jake was younger than I envisioned, maybe twenty-three or so, but he sure looked shifty: slicked-back dark hair, squinty eyes, and bushy mustache above full lips and clean-shaven face.

"Angoras," Jake said proudly. "Best haulers for the tight mountain passes."

"What 'bout our wood?" the captain barked. "Ye only half-filled."

"Uh, uh..., seems I under-calculated."

"Is that right?" the captain said. "Then, remove half ye load and get those goats outta here too."

"Hold on," Jake said, hemming and hawing. "You have enough wood to get us to Skagway. And if you can wait until I sell my goods, I can make arrangements there for more wood. In fact, I'll throw in another half-load for good measure."

The captain scratched his chin as he gnawed on Jake's proposal. "Sign a note guaranteein' ye offer," the captain said, "and only half gets unloaded in Skagway until our holds are full."

"You got a deal," Jake said, coming toward the captain with his hand extended for a handshake. The captain waved him off and headed to the pilothouse.

I gawked at the captain in disbelief and then I hurried to him. "Maybe we should rethink this."

"Too late fer that. Half is better than nothin' and we got it fer free. And if we do get more wood in Skagway, then we're the better fer it."

"It sounds as if you doubt he'll come through."

"Not countin' on nothin'." Before he walked into the pilothouse, he motioned to the bow. "What's ye sister doin' out here? Get her below."

When I reached Wilmina she was on her knees poking her fingers into a cage. "Don't do that," I said.

Jake walked up and stood beside me. "They're friendly, but *not* picky eaters so watch your fingers."

I grabbed Wilmina's sleeve. "Come on. Time for you to rejoin Viorene in the galley."

She shook her arm loose and looked up at Jake. "What are their names?"

Jake squatted down next to her and pointed from cage to cage. "That's Hillard—he's the leader. Then there's Horace, Howie, Huey, Hildy, Hannah, and Holga."

"All *H's,*" she remarked. "I love goats."

"Do you now?" he said, twisting one side of his mustache. "Tell you what, if you're willing to care for their upkeep, I'll put you in charge of them."

"You will?"

"Yep, but that includes scooping up their poop."

"And I can feed them too?"

"All you want," he said, standing up.

"No," I told him. "You're in charge of these goats." I grasped onto Wilmina's arm again and pulled her to the pilothouse. She plopped down onto the front bench and scowled. After I explained Jake's trickery to the captain, he shook his head.

"Best we try to get along," he said.

"So you're okay if I watch after the goats?" Wilmina said, but she didn't wait for his answer. Instead, she leaped up and raced out the door. I knew right then that we'd lost the fight.

I sat down and crossed my arms. "Doesn't seem right to be using the *Irene* as a barge. And that Jake is a snollygoster. He tricked Wilmina into cleaning up after those goats." I wanted to add that I thought that he had tricked the captain too, but I didn't.

"Better get past all that," the captain said. "We needed wood. It's an honorable way to earn it. Ye dad would agree."

"I suppose," I said, but deep down I wasn't so sure if that's how Daddy would've viewed it, any of it. Ever since he'd gone missing, I had wanted to find him so bad that I hadn't thought beyond what could be faced: unknown waters, rough-neck towns, and unscrupulous men. But the worst for all of it was disgracing the *Irene* with goats that smelled worse than a thousand peeled onions, especially when they pooped.

Alaska State Library - Historical Collections

Icebergs at Juneau, Alaska
(Steamboat in Gastineau Channel; Juneau in background)

*(Courtesy of Alaska State Library, Historical Collections,
William R. Norton Photo Collection, ca. 1890-1920
ASL-P226-239)*

CHAPTER 2
GASTINEAU CHANNEL
ALASKA

AFTER TWO DAYS OF SAILING, Juneau would
be our next stop. As the captain napped, Jake sat on
the front bench and I steered the *Irene* through
plummeting cliffs, so close that I was certain if I
reached out I could touch them. Holding my breath,
I prayed the rock face wouldn't breach our keel.

When the channel widened, relief washed
through me until I spotted icebergs floating in the
distance like scattered blue clouds. I glanced at Jake.
"Is that ice?"

"Yep," Jake replied in an unalarmed manner.
"Breaks off from Mendenhall Glacier when the
weather warms."

"Isn't it dangerous?" I said, now noticing that we
were sailing through chunks. "Maybe we should head
to shore and wait until the tide carries some away."

He stepped toward me. "Move aside. I know
these waters. I'll take it from here."

I reluctantly let go of the wheel and headed to the
window for a closer look. My stomach wrenched as I
watched the ice chunks get larger and larger.

"Watch out," I screamed, but not before we
slammed into one the size of a small island.

CRASH!

The *Irene* jolted.

Slivered ice flew across the deck.

"What was that?" the captain said, sitting up.

"We hit ice," I said.

The captain stumbled to his feet and hurried to the helm. Grabbing the wheel, he gave Jake a disgusted look. "Ye should've never attempted this."

"It's nothing," Jake said, but I could see by his face that he was rattled and so was the captain.

Captain Murphy opened the throttle and shifted the forward-reverse lever back and forth.

Our engine faltered.

"*Sput...sput...sput....*"

I shook my head and caught Jake's glare.

"You're making too much of this," Jake said.

"Ye better hope that's the case," Captain Murphy responded. "Get out there with the gaff and try to divert it. Aggie, get Billy up here to help."

As Jake stomped out the door, I climbed down the ladder into the galley. Wilmina greeted me.

"Is that an iceberg?" she asked.

"Yes." I looked at Billy. He and Viorene were on the bunks staring out the portholes. "The captain wants you to help Jake out on the deck."

"Okay," he said, sliding off the bunk. He grabbed his coat and hurried toward the stairs.

"This is exciting. I'm going too," Wilmina said.

"No. You and Viorene stay below. I'll let you know when it's safe to come up."

SCRAPING AGAINST OUR HULL, the bluish iceberg creaked and moaned. Billy and Jake stabbed their gaffs into the berg, and then pushed with their hands. Back and forth, they tried.

Captain Murphy opened the pilothouse door and walked out. "Save ye energy, boys. Careful where ye walk. Don't need no one breakin' a leg." He hobbled over to the gunwale and eyeballed the berg.

I followed him out, but within two steps, I realized that the deck was as slippery as a slimy fish. It surprised me that the captain didn't fall. I stopped, grabbed the broom, and inched outside again. Carefully, I swept ice into piles, picked up the larger spiked pieces, and tossed them overboard. Closer I got to the iceberg, goose bumps popped all over my arms, neck, and clear down my spine.

When I heard footsteps, I turned and narrowed my eyes at my sisters. "I told you to stay below. It's slippery out here."

Wilmina shrugged, then baby-stepped past me to the captain, leaned over the gunwale, and touched the berg. "It's the same color as Grandma's sapphire brooch."

"Brrrr," Virorene said, rubbing her arms. "I tried to stop Wilmina, but you know how stubborn she gets." I nodded. Viorene glanced at the iceberg and bit her lip. "What a dangerous situation. I'll wait in the pilothouse." She slowly turned and balanced with extended arms all the way to the door.

"The goats," Wilmina blurted. "I have to see if they're all right." She skidded past me and I tried to catch her sleeve, but she was too fast. Moments later, two goats raced across the deck, slipping and sliding like newborn calves.

"Stop, Hillard. Stop, Horace," Wilmina yelled, chasing behind them. She reached Hillard first; he was larger and slower. She clutched onto his neck and held him in place, but Horace slipped toward the stern and, before any of us could react, disappeared. "Oh no," Wilmina shrieked.

Jake stomped over to Wilmina. "How'd they get out?"

Whenever Wilmina got excited, she'd lisp, replacing her *Ssss* and *Zsss* with *th*. "I'm *thorry*. They looked *thcared*. I opened their cage to hug them."

Jake gritted his teeth and shook his head, then grabbed Hillard at the nape and dragged him back to the cages.

"What about Horace?" she asked through tears.

"Dead," he said in an angry tone. "Water's too cold. Probably be eaten by an orca."

I hurried to her. "Come on," I told her, pulling her toward the pilothouse.

Billy called out. "Over here. The goat fell into the lazaret." The lazaret was a five-foot-deep open storage built into the aft deck.

Wilmina gasped, and before I knew what was happening, she was halfway to Billy.

"How is he?" I asked, carefully stepping toward them and looking down at the curly-haired goat, baaing and stumbling as if trying to get out.

"A bit stunned, but no blood," said Billy. "Fell into the nets."

Jake, now at our side, knelt down and examined the goat. "Might as well leave him here until we dock."

The captain walked over, frustration showed on his face. "Got bigger issues than those goats," he barked. His eyes fixed on Wilmina. "Get in the pilothouse, now. The rest of ye come with me."

As I stood next to the captain, he studied the iceberg again. "Only hope is to pull away from it." He looked at me. "Go check our draw."

The *Irene* had a five-foot draw—the boat's depth from the water surface to her lowest point. Daddy had painted a red line, showing where the water should *never* go below or we might go aground and get stuck.

I leaned over the gunwale. "I can see from here that the water is still above the mark."

"Good," he said. "While the boys and I keep watch on the iceberg, get the engine warmed. When I tell ye, open the throttle, put her in reverse, then forward. Keep doin' that until I say stop."

"You want me to handle the helm? Wouldn't it be better if you or Jake were at the wheel?"

"Don't get all chicken liver on me now."

How'd he know my stomach quivered like raw liver?

As I stood at the wheel, I shifted the lever back and forth with shaking hands. The cylinders hissed and the piston rods pumped up and down. The *Irene* rocked and rocked and the iceberg scratched and groaned. Not long after, the captain opened the door.

"Aggie-girl, ye did good," the captain said, "but looks like we may have sprung a leak. Move her slow and keep the rudder straight. Jake said Douglas Island is at the next bend."

"All right," I said, panic pulsing through me. "Have you checked the galley?" I was now recalling the *Molly Mae,* the captain's boat that had sprung leaks in its galley and later sank with me at the helm.

"Aye," he said. "Saw no signs of damage, just the outside hull."

I nodded and smiled, trying to show reassurance, but knew first hand that leaks could spring at any time.

While Wilmina stood at the front window with binoculars, Viorene sat on the front bench and bit her fingernails. "The *Irene* could sink, couldn't she?" Viorene said.

"I'm already a jumble of nerves," I told her. "Please don't add more hysterics."

"Aggie," Wilmina interrupted.

"No talking. I need to concentrate."

Grasping the wheel, my hands sweated and shook something fierce. I looked at my sisters, took a deep breath, and slowly steered the boat. I knotted up again. Sweat beaded on my brow. With every creak and moan, my heart thumped even harder.

After a bit, the captain came through the door. "Let me at the wheel."

I stepped to the side, and staggered over to the side bench and sat. Suddenly, banging repeated at even spurts.

Bang, bang, bang.

Viorene covered her ears. "What is that? Are we sinking?"

"Hush," the captain told her. "It ain't the boat."

I looked at my sisters and placed my finger to my lips. "Shhh...."

Wilmina jumped up. "I see a dock."

"Aye," the captain remarked. "Must be Douglas Island. Jake said it was close."

Approaching a piling, the captain cut the engine and the *Irene* drifted toward the dock. I yanked on the steam whistle cord, pulling it up and down as it shrilled. Several men raced to the end of the dock. Jake and Billy threw them the lines.

The captain sighed and pulled a rag out of his shirt pocket, wiped his forehead, and dabbed his face. Soon as the *Irene* was secured to the dock, the captain hobbled toward me, sat down on the bench, and patted my leg.

"We made it, Aggie-girl." His face showed relief, but still looked strained.

"Yes," I said, exhaling a deep breath.

Jake and Billy came through the door. "It's only a small leak," Jake said. "The tugboat crew went for lumber. They do this type of ice-berg repairs all the time."

The captain nodded. He appeared too exhausted to speak.

Viorene cleared her throat. "I still hear banging." Jake glanced at her. "That's the stamp mill at Treadwell. It crushes ore to extract the gold. Those hammers weigh a 1,020 pounds and drop ninety-eight times a minute."

"Treadwell?" said Wilmina.

"Treadwell mines," he said explaining that it started as a single gold claim but was now a bustling community of workers and families. "Has stores, mess halls, bunkhouses, and even a marching band," he added.

"How can people stand the pounding?" Viorene asked, still holding her hands over her ears.

"They get used to it. Good work for the miners who lost everything at the Klondike. I even went down in the tunnels to dig. Only lasted a day."

"How close are we to Juneau?" the captain said.

"Just across the channel."

The captain nodded. "Kids," he said, "we lucked out. If that iceberg been much bigger, we could've lost the *Irene.*"

Right then, the sinking of the captain's boat, the *Molly Mae,* popped into my head again. Pressing my hands against my queasy stomach, I raced out the door to the gunwale, leaned over toward the water, and lost my breakfast.

CHAPTER 3
JUNEAU

WITH THE *IRENE* repaired, we sailed to Juneau and docked. Exhaustion had overtaken all of us, but hunger had won out. As we followed Jake up the planked streets that extended right up to storefront doors, same as cobblestone ones did in big cities, I admired the detail added to the buildings. Some were two-story with white-trimmed windows. Others even had scalloped eaves and spacious porches.

Viorene pointed to a colorful sign on a large building. "Does that say music hall?"

"Yep. Good singers too," Jake told her as he opened the door into the local eatery.

Sure enough, soon as we walked inside, we drew attention. "Looky there," a miner said. "Ain't they cute." Everyone gawked at us—several miners, a man and woman, and a group of women in fancy hats.

"Go," Captain Murphy said, motioning to a table in the corner.

The waitress recognized Jake right off. "Hello Jake," she said smiling. "It's been awhile. Are you heading up to Skagway?"

"Yep," he said.

"We don't see many young girls in these parts," she said. "Especially blonde ones."

"Just passin' through," Captain Murphy said.

We all ordered the same thing. Or should I say, Captain Murphy didn't give us a choice. Flapjacks and eggs. "Sticks to the bones," he said. He later asked the waitress about the *Claudina*, the boat we knew Daddy had sailed on, but she said no ships had come through for over a week. After breakfast, Jake announced that he was going for milk.

"Milk?" the captain said.

"Dairies all through these parts. Milk's a real luxury. Figured I could scrape ice off a berg, fill up your fish hold, and haul at least ten vats."

"Thought the plan was to pick up a few supplies and get on our way?" the captain said. "I want out of here."

"Only be gone four hours or so. If Billy comes, might go faster."

"All right," the captain said. "Take Aggie too."

The captain and my sisters headed back to the boat, Billy and Jake to the stable, and I went to the general store to inquire about Daddy. The waitress could have been wrong about no boats stopping and I didn't see the harm in asking if anyone had seen a man fitting Daddy's description: early thirties, about six-foot, blond, and muscular. The shopkeeper laughed, "You think I pay attention to any of those scrubby prospectors, they all look the same to me."

I continued up the dirt street and poked my head into two saloons and looked around, asked at the blacksmith shop and the music hall too. When I saw

Billy at the stable door, I hurried over just as Jake drove out a wagon.

Two ladies dressed in long cloaks and fancy hats waved for Jake to stop. I recognized them from the diner.

"Whoa," Jake hollered, pulling on the reins as the women approached.

"Overheard you say you're sailing to Skagway," the taller woman said. "Have room for two more?"

"We're awful crammed," I said, but I got ignored by both Jake and the women.

"Twenty-five dollars. Each," Jake said.

"Want it now?" she asked. After he nodded, she reached into her pocket.

Jake extended his hand and took her money. "Be at the boat in two hours. It's the *Irene*."

"Will do," the woman said and they walked away.

I looked at Jake. "We never agreed to take people. And that was far too much to ask."

"Captain said he'd transport in exchange for wood. Consider them part of my load."

"We'll see about that," I said. "I'm going back to the boat to talk to the captain now."

Closer I got to the dock, the louder the pounding from the stamp mill. After I climbed aboard, I found my sisters and Captain Murphy inside the pilothouse, huddled around the back bench.

"Captain, gotta problem. We need to talk."

"We got a situation too."

When he moved to one side, I saw something wrapped in a blanket. I stepped closer.

Tiny arms and legs flailed and kicked.

"Is that a baby?" I whispered.

"Got left when we went to town," Viorene said.

"Why would someone leave us a baby?"

"No idea," the captain said. "Best we wait fer Jake to return, then come up with a plan."

"Speaking of Jake, he signed on two ladies to travel with us. He already took their money."

"Guess we'll have to make room."

"That's it? Shouldn't we say no?"

"Dealin' with this baby is more important than takin' two more people along."

CHAPTER 4
JUNEAU

VIORENE HAD WRAPPED the baby's ears to protect them from the noisy stamp-mill hammering, then changed her diaper and fed her the last of the bottled milk that had been left for her. We stuffed a goose quilt inside a wooden box, put the baby inside, and covered her with her blanket.

"It's a blessing that Jake is bringing back more milk," Viorene said.

"Doubt he'll want to share it," I remarked.

"He won't have a choice," she replied.

"I better get to the pilothouse and prepare for our guests," I told my sisters.

When I got to the upper deck, I saw that the ladies had already come aboard. Without their hats, I got a better view.

The one talking to the captain had flaming red hair down to her waist, a round face, and was full-bodied at every angle. The other one seemed younger—I figured no more than eighteen—and was the beauty of the two. Thin with an oval face, she had silky black hair tied up in a bun.

I walked over and stood next to the dark-haired girl.

"Hello. I'm Lillie Mae," she said. She had pearly white teeth—pretty as Viorene's—and deep blue eyes.

"I'm Aggie," I told her.

"No one said anythin' about trunks," the captain barked. He turned to me and scowled.

"I didn't know either," I admitted, "but we might be able to make room over by the cages."

The captain sighed. "See what ye can do," he told me, and then looked at the redhead again. "If it don't fit, some of it will be stayin' behind."

The captain and the women followed me over to the cages. After I moved the buckets and slid two feed barrels to one side, the captain motioned for two men to bring the trunks aboard.

"Lucky fer ye," he told the women, "she found room." He turned to me. "Take 'em below and get 'em settled."

The redhead frowned. "Not me. I don't do well with confinement."

"We'll give ye a pail," the captain said.

She glared at the captain. "We paid good money for proper accommodations."

"Didn't pay me. Take it or leave it."

Lillie Mae clasped her friend's hand and turned to the captain. "We appreciate your hospitality. Come along," she told her redheaded friend, following me to the hatch, down the stairs and into the galley.

"Better than I expected," the redhead said, "but no promises on not getting sick."

I pointed to my bed. "You can rest there. If you do get queasy, climb the stairs to the top step and look out at the water. It'll relax you. I do it all the time."

"That old geezer could learn manners from you," she said. She extended her hand to me. "I'm Sadie."

Before I could give her my name, Wilmina piped up. "She's Aggie. I'm Wilmina. You sure are pretty. I've never seen such wild hair."

"Wilmina, get over here," Viorene instructed.

I could tell from Viorene's tone she wasn't pleased to have the ladies aboard. Luckily, the pounding from the stamp mill masked the annoyance in her voice.

"Wilmina didn't mean anything bad," I added.

"No bother to me," Sadie said. "I'm famous for my hair. My stage name is *Raging Red Sadie*. Lillie Mae is *The Raven.*"

"Stage name?" Viorene said.

"We're songbirds. Singers at the music hall."

Wilmina gasped. "Will you sing for us?"

"Only if you agree to join in, but let's wait until we get out to sea," said Sadie, sitting on the edge of my bed next to Lillie Mae.

Wilmina plopped down and sat on the floor in front of them.

"What brings you girls to these parts?" Sadie asked.

"We're looking for our daddy," Wilmina said. "He sailed to Alaska on a schooner."

"So, he's a prospector?"

"No, he'd never take interest in that," I said. "We're guessing he's part of the crew."

Just then, the baby wailed, louder than the pounding from the stamp mill.

"A baby?" Sadie said.

Viorene cleared her throat. "Someone left her in the pilothouse while we were in town. Do you have any ideas on who she belongs to?"

"Lots of desperate girls in these parts," Sadie said.

Viorene stared at her. "But to leave her on a boat with strangers?"

"Must've seen you girls in town and knew you'd take care of her."

"We can't keep her. What should we do?"

"Don't' know and glad I don't have to figure it out."

WHEN JAKE AND BILLY RETURNED, they fished ice out of the water, put it in our fish hold, and set twelve milk vats inside. Jake was indifferent when he heard about the baby. "None of my concern," he had said. Not Billy. He couldn't wait to get a glimpse and rushed down to the galley to see her.

I pointed to the vats. "Need one of those."

"Only one," Jake said. "After that, use goat's milk."

"You told me that Angoras weren't good producers."

"They trickle some. You'll have to milk all three females to get a cup."

"Then what? Let the baby starve?"

"I didn't sign on to lose money."

"This problem is as much yours as ours. You said anyone added was part of your load. We need to find her parents. Shouldn't we ask around town?"

"Won't do any good. More than likely they're long gone. Only hope is to come across missionaries or a family, but might have to pay them to take her. Too bad we can't find the mother. Then we could sell them both to a prospector."

"That's your answer?"

"Forget about the baby for now. We need to get moving."

The more I was around Jake, the less I liked him. It made me wonder if his word had merit in Wrangell when it came time to collect our remaining promised wood. But what choice did we have but to trust him? Need to keep my thoughts to myself, I decided. But for thirteen hours? At eight knots an hour, that's how long I calculated it'd take to reach Skagway. But I had to try.

On my sixth trip down to the engine room, I heard singing, hurried to the galley doorway and listened.

It was Sadie, belting out *Oh! Susanna,* with different words than I knew. *"I'll be going to Alaska with a wash pan on my knee."*

Wilmina and Billy clapped along. Viorene tapped her foot as she held the baby, feeding her a bottle. Two bottles had been left with the baby and Viorene always kept one nearby.

Soon as Sadie finished, we all clapped. Lillie Mae stood next, clasped her hands, and took a deep breath. When she opened her mouth, high-pitched operatic notes flowed out. Mostly *ah's* and *oh's*, each higher than the last. I imagined angels would sound like her. When she finished, she curtsied.

"Your voice is pure heaven," Viorene said.

She smiled. "Thank you."

"I could listen to you for hours," I added.

Sadie smirked, but in a fun way. "What about me?"

I grinned. "You were good too."

"Maybe one of you girls has the making of a star," Sadie said. "Who wants to sing first?"

I shook my head. "Need to get to work."

Billy followed me into the engine room. "They sure are fun. Never met anyone like 'em."

We listened as Wilmina sang, "*Skip, skip, skip to my Lou...*"

"My voice isn't much better. It's Viorene who can sing, but she won't do it in front of them. Only place I've ever heard her is in church."

When I got to the pilothouse, I found myself humming Wilmina's tune. I kept it low so as not to wake the captain. Even with the occasional crying of the baby, being in the galley seemed to be more enjoyable than time in the pilothouse with Jake. I limited my talking by looking out the window. When he wasn't at the helm, he sat on the side bench with his notebook, adding up figures.

"If I charge an extra ten dollars for the goats to pack supplies for the prospectors up and back, I can make eighty dollars more."

"Is money all that interests you?"

"Isn't it what everyone wants? Why do you think these prospectors are digging for gold? Or shopkeepers selling goods? Truth is farmers farm to make money."

"Farmers do it to survive and raise a family."

"Not all of them. You're just too young to understand the real world."

He was wrong, I did understand. When we fished, I liked catching an extra-large one for the money it brought, but something about him didn't seem right to me.

"How are the ladies doing below? Thought I heard singing."

"You did," I answered curtly.

"You seem perturbed. What's up with you?"

"Your remark about selling the baby didn't set well with me."

"You don't understand Alaska. You're just a kid."

"What does understanding it have to do with right and wrong?"

"That baby is of no use to anyone. It's already a burden taking my milk. If someone showed an interest, you bet I'd sell it."

"Take the wheel," I said. "I'm going below to check on the boiler."

On my way to the engine room, I passed the galley, peeked in, and saw Viorene and Lillie Mae sitting on my bunk, talking. Sadie, Billy, and Wilmina were at the table, playing cards.

"Wildman Jack," Sadie said as she put down a card. "Time to use the bucket."

"You don't have to use a bucket," Wilmina said. "We have a privy in the pilothouse."

Sadie got up and approached me. "Hope I don't run into that old geezer."

Even though I'd never call the captain that, it humored me. "Don't worry. He's fast asleep. Soon as you step inside the pilothouse, the privy door is on the left."

"What is it? Another bucket?"

"No, it's a pull-rope toilet."

I explained that the privy resembled an outhouse, and with a pull of the rope, the collected rainwater from the roof traveled down to the bowl, filled it up, and then flushed it out to sea. "Wish me luck," she said, heading up the stairs. I smiled and walked into the engine room.

After I checked the water gauge on the boiler, I opened the furnace door, pulled out a two-by-four from the woodpile, and threw it in. Just then, something rustled behind the woodpile. A rat, I figured. I quickly closed the firebox door, grabbed another board, and tiptoed to where I heard the noise. I held the board like a bat, ready to whack a beady-eyed vermin.

A foot slid out.

I jumped back.

"Whoever you are, come out."

I stood back, but didn't lower the board until I saw a young blonde girl crawl out. "Who are you? What're you doing here?"

She slowly stood, and then spoke in broken English. "Run away."

Just then, Sadie's voice echoed from behind me. "I'm guessing you're the baby's mother?" she said.

The girl looked at Sadie and nodded.

Sadie walked closer. "What's your story?"

Tears welled in the girl's eyes. "My husband killed, logging. Only have Catrine now."

"That's your baby?" Sadie said.

She nodded again. "My husband and I from Sweden, no other family here."

"And no husband means debt," Sadie replied.

"I looked for work, but the saloon owner claimed me as his mail-order bride. No one would speak up or help. I ran away."

Sadie must have heard my gasp, because she turned to me. "Girls are jewels in these parts.

Especially a pretty one like her." She looked at the girl. "Is the man named Hanes?"

"Yaaa."

"Don't blame you for running. I wouldn't want that old wind-bag Wilbert Hanes for a husband, either. Reminds me of a two-hundred-pound seal. Greasy black hair, spiky whiskers, and he barks like one too."

The girl snickered. "My husband was very handsome and young. Not old like Mr. Hanes."

"How have you been surviving?" Sadie asked.

"A farmer's wife caught me stealing food from her shed. Then she started helping. At night we'd sleep in her shed, and during the day hide in the woods. She saw girls get off your boat and rushed to tell me."

"Good woman."

"Yaaa."

I looked at Sadie. "We have another concern—Jake. He said he'd sell the baby if he found a buyer. Better price if he had the baby's mother too. So, you know if he finds out about the saloon owner, he'll cash in on that."

"No," the girl cried. "I don't want to go back."

Sadie touched the girl's arm. "Don't worry. We'll keep you both safe." Sadie turned to me. "Better get this girl hidden."

"My name is Inga. Can I see my baby, please?"

Sadie nodded. "Wait here."

Viorene carried the baby into the engine room and handed her to the girl. Wilmina, Lillie Mae, and Billy followed and formed a half-circle of smiles.

Lillie Mae put her arm around Viorene. "Warms your heart." Viorene smiled and looked lovingly at the baby, but I wasn't surprised about that. She always had a fondness for little ones.

"This is Inga," I announced, "and her baby Catrine. They need our help, but this has to be kept secret, especially from Jake."

"From the captain too?" asked Viorene.

"At least until we hash out a plan," I said. "He doesn't need more worries. Jake and our low wood supply are enough."

Viorene nodded. "What do we need to do?"

Her response surprised me. Ever since we started this trip, she had turned sour on every idea I had proposed. I was pleased to see the old Viorene back, even if it was just a glimpse.

"First, we get Inga fed, then hidden. I'm thinking they can stay in the boiler shed."

"Absolutely not," said Viorene. "It's too hot in there when the boiler's burning."

"What do you suggest?"

"Why can't she stay in the galley with us? That way, she can have Catrine with her. Besides, Jake's only been down here once." Viorene glanced around at the others. "We could take turns guarding the stairs."

Alaska State Library - Historical Collections

Skagway, Alaska, 1898

*(Courtesy of Alaska State Library, Historical Collections,
Frank H. Nowell Photo Collection
ASL-P48-150)*

CHAPTER 5
SKAGWAY

SNOW-CROWNED PEAKS FRAMED both sides of Skagway, which was butted below in a narrow valley. After we anchored in the channel, I looked toward Skagway again. It was as described—noisy and lawless. That was evident from the street fights we witnessed with our binoculars. We heard gunshots too, hoping they were fired into the air.

The wind howled across the long channel and watercraft of every size and shape—schooners, scows, rafts, and canoes—bobbed and creaked. A long dock on pilings, a good half-mile away, stretched along the waterfront, and farther down was a city of white tents.

Wilmina jumped up and down, pulled on my sleeve. "Daddy's *th*chooner," she lisped. "There's the carving of Mama."

When we first saw the *Claudina* sailing out of Port Townsend, we saw Daddy standing on her deck. Our binoculars confirmed it. A shipyard worker said that someone named John had carved the figurehead. We later learned that Daddy was going by that name. The figurehead looked just like Mama: black flowing hair, rosy cheeks and lips, and her lopsided smile.

I hugged Wilmina. "What a happy day this is."

"I'll let Viorene know," she said, racing off to the galley.

I hurried to the pilothouse. "Captain, the *Claudina's* here."

He smiled. "Good to know it wasn't a wasted trip."

"Can we row over to it now? Please."

"Get the ladies ashore first."

USING THE WINCH and pulley, Billy and I lowered our dinghy into the water and then pushed the folded-up rope ladder over the edge. I turned when I heard footsteps. It was my sisters with Sadie and Lillie Mae. Sadie gathered me into a hug.

"What a remarkable young girl you are," she said. "Don't be a stranger." She turned to my sisters and hugged them too. "You've all been a delight."

"It sure was fun meeting you," Wilmina said, squeezing Sadie's waist again. "I'll miss you."

Sadie smiled down at my sister and stroked her hair. When she looked at me, I saw wetness in her eyes.

Jake brushed past us and onto the ladder, then hollered, "Let's get going." Halfway down, he let go and landed in the boat. It wobbled side to side.

Sadie placed both feet onto a rung before stepping down to another. When she got to the bottom rung, Jake helped her into the dinghy. Once Lillie Mae got within Jake's reach, he grabbed her waist and lifted her down. In my opinion, he held on longer to her than he should have. Sadie noticed too.

"We'll send a ferry barge for our trunks tomorrow," Sadie hollered. "Don't forget to visit us."

"Will do," I said. I looked at Jake. "Hurry back, I need to use the dinghy."

"Not until I unload all my supplies first."

Sadie glanced at him, then up at me. "Girl, climb down here now. We'll row over to the schooner first."

Jake glared at her. "What?"

"You heard me," she said. "Won't be but a few minutes to row over to that ship."

I turned to my sisters. "Hope you don't mind if I go without you." I hurried down the ladder. Soon as I sat at the stern, I picked up a set of oars. Jake's irritated stare told me to limit conversation with him.

"You're not strong enough to row a filled boat," he snapped.

"Can, with help. Lockstep to my strokes." And it appeared that my rowing surprised him. In fact, I was better than he was.

When we reached the *Claudina*, Sadie called out to a man, who was leaning against the rail. "Yoo-hoo, young man."

He looked down at her.

Sadie pointed to the prow. "Need to talk to the gentleman who carved that woman on your ship."

"Not here. Took his pay and headed off. Probably halfway up the mountain by now."

"Thank you," she said. She looked at me with a sympathetic smile. "Sorry, Aggie."

I nodded, then hollered up to the man. "How long ago did he leave?"

"Least four days ago. Who are you ladies?"

"Songbirds at the Skagway music hall," Sadie answered. "Ask for Sadie and I'll get you front-row seats."

When we reached the dock, Jake tied on to a piling, climbed out of the dinghy, and extended his hand to Lillie Mae, then helped Sadie out. He jumped back in, untied the boat and sat. I was still waving goodbye when he pulled back on his oars. It caught me off balance and I dropped my oar into the water.

"Alert a person before you to pull," I told him. I leaned over the gunwale, trying to fish my oar out of the water, but he continued rowing. "My daddy made that oar."

He shrugged. "You can buy another one in town."

After we tied onto the *Irene,* I followed him up the ladder and was greeted at the taffrail by my sisters, the captain, and Billy.

"Did you see Daddy?" Wilmina said, words tumbling out faster than she could take a breath. "Where is he? What'd he say? When's he coming?"

I had intended on discussing what to say with the captain first, but now being flooded with questions, I froze. "Uh....," I repeated several times.

"What's wrong?" Viorene said.

"He did arrive, but he left the schooner four days ago."

"Where'd he go?" she said.

I looked at the captain, hoping he'd say something to ease their minds.

"Bet he got gold fever," Captain Murphy said.

"That's not Daddy's nature," I blurted in a defending tone. "He never believed in searching for lost treasures."

He nodded at me, then glanced at my sisters. "Aye. We'll find him in town. His sea legs probably needed a stretch on land."

I smiled at him. He grinned back and nodded, but I could tell by his face that he believed that Daddy was long gone.

THE NEXT MORNING the captain insisted Viorene stay aboard. "One of ye has to fetch me coffee and tend to the baby," he had said.

Viorene didn't argue. She had already agreed to stay aboard. One of us had to keep up the charade of watching after the baby. I feared if the captain knew about Inga, he'd worry himself into a pother. And if Jake found out about her, he'd find a way to sell her, trade her, or stir up a reward.

"Fine by me," Viorene said. "Last thing I need to see is a dusty town full of prospectors."

Jake had commissioned a raft owner to haul his supplies to the dock and put them on a wagon, but left the goats on our boat. Before he and Billy climbed onto the raft, I brought up the wood he owed us. "Will you be bringing back a full load of wood?"

He glared at me. "This is between me and the captain."

"The agreement was the wood before you fully unloaded."

"You'll get your wood."

"When?"

"When I say so, how's that?"

The Captain interjected. "Aggie, let it go fer now. Ye girls better get goin' while the town's still asleep. And be careful rowin'. Lots of floatin' crafts out there."

SKAGWAY DIDN'T APPEAR much different than the other Alaskan towns. It had one long dirt road as its main street edged by wood-framed buildings, and more respectable businesses than expected: bank, tin shops, general store, telegraph office, and a volunteer fire department, to name a few. But then there was saloon after saloon after saloon and dance halls, all with painted posters plastered everywhere we looked advertising the oddest things: sword swallowers, fire dancers, and even a dancing bear. The largest painting displayed mountain peaks, a red wagon pulled by horses, and smiling prospectors. That poster took up the whole outside wall of the building and advertised:

White Pass
All-wagon Trail
Easiest route to the Klondike

A tiny bell jingled as we entered the general store. "Look at the recommended supplies for gold seekers." I recited the pinned-up list next to the door: "Cornmeal 50 lbs, flour 400 lbs, bacon 200 lbs. The list goes on and on."

"Most pack it on their backs," a man's voice said. "Ones, who can afford it, buy horses to pull their load."

I turned around. "I didn't see you there, sir."

"I was in the back. Heard you when you came in. Is your kin hiking the trail?"

"No," I said. I reached into my pocket for our family photo. Taken three years back, Daddy wore his captain's hat and navy-blue pea coat. Mama, her black dress and jeweled broach. We three girls had on our Sunday best—blue-flowered dresses, black tights, and oversized, matching bows fastened to the back of our hair. Not that color mattered. The photo was black and white.

"We're looking for this man," I said, tapping the photo. "He came to Skagway about four days ago off of a sailing ship. Have you seen him?"

The man studied the picture, then shook his head. "Go to the tin shop and ask there. It's the first place a stampeder goes for supplies."

At the tin shop, we were forced to stand in a line. More than once, prospectors whacked their heads on the hanging tin debris, setting off a clamor of banging pots and pans, followed by a string of swear words. Each time, I quickly covered Wilmina's ears.

"Let's check the time again." I pulled out Daddy's pocket watch. It took us close to an hour to reach the counter.

"What're you buying?" the shopkeeper said.

"Nothing," I said.

"Then get out of line," he demanded. "It's already trailing out the door."

"Half-dollar, for a moment of your time?"

He gave me a quizzical look. "What's this about?"

I placed our family photo on the counter. "Have you seen this man?"

He picked it up. "Hmm. So many come through here." Then, he looked at me. "Huh," he said. "There was a Swedish-looking man with a square jaw, just like yours. It struck me odd that he was clean-shaven, but it made me notice his face."

A prospector hollered from the back. "What's the hold up?"

The shopkeeper looked up. "Wait your turn, they're paying customers."

"How long ago?" I asked.

"At least three days. He was heading up White Pass. Handed me the list to outfit him. That's all I got for you, kid."

I reached into my pocket and slid my half-dollar across the counter to him. "Thank you."

He pushed the coin back. "Keep it." He looked past me. "Next?"

I slipped the money back into my pocket, grabbed Wilmina's hand, and zigzagged us through the crowd, out the door.

"What now?" Wilmina said.

"We can't go into any saloons without a male escort. The captain was firm on that, so we might as well check on Billy."

"What about visiting Sadie and Lillie Mae?" she asked.

"They work late hours, doubt if they'd be awake. But maybe tomorrow we can."

When we walked into the stable, Billy was kneeling at a sled, organizing supplies. Except for being three times longer, the sled reminded me of a wood-carved baby cradle. Longer than wide, it had horizontal open slats along both sides, a railing atop, but instead of rockers for feet, it had ski-like iron runners. Two pull ropes were at the front and wheelbarrow-like handles on the back.

"That's an awful big heap." I pointed to supplies in the corner. "How's it all going to fit?"

"Takin' a wagon and a mule and leavin' the smaller sled behind," Billy said. "Jake worked a forty-sixty split with the stable owner. Owner was happy for the forty percent."

"So he doesn't need the goats?" Wilmina said.

"Still does, for the larger sled."

"But sleds need snow," she said.

"Not this one. It's built for mud, grass, snow and ice. Wouldn't want goopy mud, but according to Jake, the path's hardened enough not to be an issue."

"Sounds like you're going up the mountain with Jake?" I said.

"The money's too good to pass up."

"What about us? You promised to help search for our Daddy. Plus, we still have work on the boat."

"Jake's payin' me twenty dollars. Maybe more, if the load increases."

"How long will you be gone?"

"At least two weeks. Might be longer."

"The captain won't be happy to hear that."

"He won't care. He's always tellin' me to have an adventure."

"That's true," I said.

I tried not to show my concern, but I questioned the captain's advice. Billy had already lived through being orphaned and forced to steal to survive. I feared Jake's negative influence might pull him back into an unlawful life.

"Any leads on your dad?" he asked.

"The shopkeeper at the tin shop recognized him."

"So he's prospecting?"

"Appears so."

"I could take your photo up the mountain and show it around."

"Suppose that'd be a good idea, but safeguard it. It's the only family photo we have." I took it out of my pocket and handed it to him.

"I'll protect it," he said, and slipped it into his inside coat pocket. "We're leavin' in the morning. Once I finish here, I'll go with you to a couple saloons."

"All right," I said. "I'll row Wilmina back to the boat and bring back food for you and Jake."

LATER, BILLY AND I checked four saloons, but all the answers were the same—*No* or *how would he look with a beard?* But the truth was, the prospectors had no interest in studying the photo. All they cared about was talking gold, drinking, or playing cards. In fact, we got scolded more than once for interrupting their poker games.

"Maybe you'll have better luck with the captain."

I nodded, but deep down I knew it'd be the same.

"Jake and I are sleeping in the stable tonight," Billy said. "I'll walk with you to the wharf."

When we got there, we saw a raft tied to the *Irene.* "Must be picking up Sadie's and Lillie Mae's trunks," I said. I turned to Billy. "Be careful on that mountain." I debated hugging him. Instead, I shook his hand. "Thanks for taking the photo with you."

"I'm anxious to meet your dad and bring him back. See you in a few weeks," he said, "and thanks for bringing the food." He waited for me to get into the dinghy and waved as I pulled my oars through the water. It made me sad watching him walk away.

Soon as I stepped aboard the *Irene*, I heard Wilmina screaming *no, no*. I raced toward her voice.

Jake had the cages harnessed, ready to be lifted off the boat, but Wilmina had climbed onto Hillard's cage and wouldn't move. Viorene pleaded, but Wilmina ignored every word.

"Get off that cage," Jake hollered.

Tears streamed down Wilmina's cheeks. Her swollen eyelids, red as ripe cherries, told me this battle had been going on for some time.

"You try," Viorene said to me, stepping back. She had the same frustrated look on her face as Captain Murphy and Jake.

"Wilmina," I said in an extra-soft tone. "It's time for Hillard to go to work."

"No. He'll be eaten by wolves. Please, Aggie. You have to help me."

"He belongs to Jake. You have to let him go."

"I won't."

"Had enough of this," Jake said. He pushed me aside, clutched Wilmina's waist, and pulled until she lost her grip on the cage. Then, he carried her over to Captain Murphy and plunked her down by his feet.

As the captain pressed on her shoulders, I

rushed over and hugged her. Wilmina squirmed, but with the captain and me locking her in place, she couldn't move.

Jake hooked the pulley to Hillard's cage and twisted the engine throttle. As the cage went up, swinging back and forth, Wilmina looked at me so sad and disbelieving, I almost cried.

"I'm sorry," I said.

The instant the cage disappeared over the gunwale and banged down onto the raft, Wilmina broke into sobs.

"Enough drama fer today," Captain Murphy said. Soon as he released her, she wiggled loose from me and raced to the stairs. The captain headed to the pilothouse.

"Between Wilmina's fit and Inga's colicky baby, I haven't had a bit of peace," Viorene said.

"Mine wasn't much better."

When Viorene and I entered the galley, we saw Inga on my bed feeding Catrine.

"Where's Wilmina?" I whispered.

She pointed to the table.

I knelt down next to the table, pulled back the curtain, and peeked in. "Wilmina? Are you all right?"

"Leave me alone," she said, talking through a pillow.

"Okay," I said. "Goodnight. I love you."

No reply.

BANG, BANG, BANG awakened me. I sat up.

We had put curtains over the portholes to blacken the room, but I saw early light fingering through, so I guessed it had to be four a.m. or about.

What now? I thought.

Viorene sat up too. "Whatever that is, it better stop before it wakes the baby."

"I'll check." I tiptoed to the stairs. Topside, I followed the sound and leaned over the gunwale. The pulley that had been hooked to the dinghy swayed in the air and was banging against the hull.

What's going on? I wondered.

I climbed down the ladder and secured the pulley. As the fog cleared from my head, I realized the dinghy hadn't gotten loose on its own. I looked toward the wharf and saw it tied to a piling. I gasped and raced up the ladder.

Moore's Wharf, Skagway, Alaska, 1898

Skagway, Alaska, 1898
(Note: Prospector tent city along the waterway)

(Courtesy of Alaska State Library, Historical Collections,
Winter and Pond Trail of '98 Photo Collection.
ASL-P21-02)

CHAPTER 6
SKAGWAY

WE SEARCHED THE PRIVY, boiler shed, even the four-foot hold in the stern's deck, but with the dinghy gone, we knew the answer.

"Heard her get up," I said. "Thought she was going to the privy. She must've waited inside it until daylight."

"Gone fer that goat," Captain Murphy said.

"That's what I figure."

"Can you imagine the uproar she's caused?" Viorene said. "Bet Jake's having a fit."

"Yes, but with the dinghy at the wharf, there's no way for me to get ashore."

"Don't fret." Captain Murphy walked over to the outside bell—the larger of two. This one Daddy had procured from a church that was replacing it because of a crack. When rung, it clanged louder than a Chinese gong.

"How's that going to help?"

"Ye'll see."

A moment later, a man at the wharf was ringing a bell back.

Captain Murphy cupped his hands around his mouth. "Need a ride to shore," he hollered to a man on a nearby raft.

"Half-dollar, one way," the man yelled back.

Viorene whispered to me. "It's the raft owner. He has a rowboat too, and taxis people to and from their boats. We saw several use his service when you were in town."

"Okay," Captain Murphy yelled to the man. He turned to me. "Get ye money."

"Should I go too?" Viorene said.

"No. Don't need two fetchin' ye sister. Besides, ye gotta watch that baby."

THE ONLY REMNANT of Jake, Billy, and the goats—empty cages, hoof prints, and skid marks on the stable's dirt floor.

I called out. "Wilminaaa...," trailing off at the end. "Please, if you hear me, please come out." I hollered until my voice grew hoarse, then I thought long and hard about where she might've gone. Sadie and Lillie Mae popped into my head.

The worry for Wilmina weighed heavy on me as I raced to the music hall. Please, please, be there I prayed under my breath. I bolted through the music-hall door and into the theater where I found Lillie Mae and Sadie sitting.

"Have you seen Wilmina? She ran away to see the goats, but Jake and Billy left early this morning."

"No, we haven't seen her," Lillie Mae said. "Are you sure she's not on the boat?"

"We checked every hiding place on the boat, even the privy."

"I'm afraid to ask," she said, "but would she have the courage to go up the mountain alone?"

That thought had entered my head, but I pushed it away until Lillie Mae put it there again.

"I see by your face," Sadie said, "she *would* do something like that."

I nodded. "Of the three of us, she never puts caution first."

"Before you panic, go back to the boat. See if she's returned," Sadie said.

"What if she hasn't?" I slumped down in a wooden chair next to Sadie. When she wrapped her arm around me, I trembled as tears spilled down my cheeks.

She stroked my hair. "We'll find her," she kept repeating. "I bet she's on the boat right now."

I pulled back and looked at her, but when I saw concern on her face, my upper lip quivered and tears welled up again.

Rowing back to the *Irene*, my stomach tightened with every stroke. If Wilmina had returned to the boat, the dinghy wouldn't have been at the wharf. When I saw Viorene and the captain standing at the gunwale looking down at me with the same concern Sadie had on her face, I knotted up again.

I quickly climbed the ladder.

"You didn't find her?" Viorene asked, panic rising in her voice.

"No."

"What about Billy or Jake? Did they have any ideas?" the captain said.

"They'd already left."

Captain Murphy sighed. "This ain't good."

"She's gone up the mountain. I know it in my gut."

Captain Murphy paced back and forth. "Crazy kid."

"Only thing I can do is go after her."

"What?" he said. "No, that's too dangerous to go alone."

"Wilmina could be alone too. And, she's four years younger than me."

"Of all times fer me to have a bum leg. Maybe we could hire someone. Get ye photo."

"I gave it to Billy, so he could look for Daddy."

"We're costing time," Viorene said. "I'm going with you. I'll gather up supplies."

"Ye can't go," the captain said. "Ye forgettin' we have a baby aboard?"

"Inga's taking care of her," Viorene blurted, then covered her mouth soon as she said it.

"Who?"

Viorene and I stared at each other, squirming in silence. Finally, I spoke.

"The baby's mother," I said sheepishly. "She stowed away in the woodpile."

"And *when* were ye goin' to tell me that?"

"We didn't want to rile you."

He shook his head. "Ohh..., ohh...," he said, snorting like a bull.

Viorene tiptoed toward the stairs.

"Viorene and I must leave now. We might be able to find Wilmina before nightfall."

"No more decisions by either one of ye. Row me to town now."

"Captain, please. We'd lose time carting you back and forth. There's so many people traveling that path, we can't get lost. And the goats should be easy to spot. But we have to get moving."

Viorene approached carrying two gunnysacks. Inga came behind her with coats and blankets draped over her arms.

"Got everything needed," Viorene said. "Canned beans, salmon, and deer jerky. Blankets and coats too."

The captain looked at Inga, threw his hands into the air, and walked away.

I whispered to Inga. "He's in a bit of a fit. Give him a minute to gather his thoughts."

He stormed back and looked at Inga square-on. "Can ye cook?"

"Yaaa," she stuttered.

"At least, ye'll be of some good." He spun around and grasped my shoulders. "I should be goin' with ye, but can't with me peg leg, but I insist ye go to the songbirds and get 'em to help. Don't defy me on that, understand?"

"All right."

"And if ye're not back in two days, I'm sendin' a search party." His voice cracked. When he looked at me again, I saw dampness in his eyes. "And Viorene, stay disguised like ye sister."

He wrapped his arms around me, kissed my cheek, and did the same to Viorene. "Be careful. I mean it." Then he hobbled toward the pilothouse, moving fast as a person with a peg leg could, and opened the door and slammed it behind him.

Viorene and Inga stuffed the blankets into two empty gunnysacks and headed to the stern. I went to get a bucket to bring along, but stopped mid-step when I viewed the captain through the pilothouse window. He sat on the front bench, slumped over, with his head cradled in his hands. When I got closer, I saw his shoulders quivering and heard his sobs. I wanted to rush in and hug him, and tell him we'd be all right. But I knew that would only make things worse.

After we lowered our supplies into the dinghy, I turned to Inga. "Give the captain a few hours, then take him coffee and a bowl of stew."

AT THE STABLE, we packed our supplies on the smaller sled that Jake and Billy had left behind. Then we headed to the music hall.

"Moves pretty easy through mud," Viorene said as we pulled the sled along.

"Let's hope it's the same on the pass."

We found Sadie on the stage singing *ahha...ahha...ahha*. She stopped when she saw us.

"We're heading up the mountain," I said.

"Not by yourselves," she said in an outraged voice. "Jimmy, get up here."

"What is it?" a young man said, coming up the stairs. Skinny as a pencil, he had sandy-colored hair and a lantern-shaped jaw.

"Ever climb White Pass to Lake Bennett?"

"Yes, tried Chilkoot Pass too. With all the back and forth relays to retrieve stashed supplies, took over twenty days to go nine miles. Finally gave up and turned back home. Lake Bennett's beyond that."

"How far?" I said.

He scratched his head. "On Chilkoot, whole trip to the lake is thirty-three miles. White's not as steep, but at least ten miles longer."

"These kids are in a fix," Sadie said. "Their eight-year-old sister's on White Pass and they need to get to her."

"It's a dangerous trail. Starts out easy, but when you get into the hills watch out."

He explained about corkscrew turns and muddy paths that edged ravines that dropped hundreds of feet down.

"It's an up-and-down trek lined with cliffs," he said. "One minute you're at a high altitude crossing through jagged rocks and ten-foot boulders, then you plummet down into swampland, soggy riverbeds, and thicket before starting up to another steep grade."

"The poster showed it as an all-wagon trail, best one to take," I said.

"Not true. Near the summit it narrows to two feet of hard-packed snow where no wagons can get through. It's nicknamed *Dead Horse Gulch* for good reason. Hundreds are strewed all along that ridge."

"We have to find Wilmina before she sees that."

Sadie picked up her purse off a chair and reached inside. "Here's twenty-five dollars." She handed it to Jimmy. "I want you to go with them."

"Sorry, it'd take days to stock up."

"They don't have days."

"Not interested," he said, giving her back her money and walking away.

"You girls stay here until I get back."

After a bit, I looked at my pocket watch. "She's been gone close to an hour. We have to go. Let's tell her goodbye."

We found Sadie's dressing room and walked in. I saw that her trunks had been delivered.

"Thought those were still on the boat."

"No," Viorene said. "Got picked up yesterday, while you and Wilmina were in town."

Feathered hats, high-top boots, and red, pink, and blue satin costumes lay scattered everywhere we looked. Sadie stood in the corner behind a partition, changing her clothes.

"Just a minute." When she stepped out from behind the divider, dressed in so many layers of cotton, wool, and lace, it surprised me she could move.

"Came to say goodbye," I said.

"Nope," she said. "I'm going with you." She lifted her skirt and showed us a pistol strapped to her leg.

White Pass Trail
(Dead Horse Gulch)

*(Courtesy of Alaska State Library, Historical Collections,
Shelby B. Combest Photo Collection, ca. 1900-1920
ASL-P308-272)*

White Pass Trail
(Man and a loaded wagon on rocky trail over White Pass summit)

*(Courtesy of Alaska State Library, Historical Collections,
Early Prints of Alaska Photo Collection, ca 1870-1920,
ASL-P297-214)*

CHAPTER 7
WHITE PASS

UNDER A FULL SUN, we slogged over swampland and the packed-down mud. Two of us pulled the sled and the other one walked ahead, picking up jagged rocks and other obstacles. Forced to rest every quarter mile or so, I looked through our binoculars every chance I got. All I ever saw a distance ahead was a grid-lock of oxen and mules or horses pulling wagons and dogs tugging sleds. Saw lots of people walking with packs strapped to their backs, but never any dark-haired little girl. And no goats, either.

My stomach wrenched and negative thoughts spun in my head: *What if we don't find her? What if she wandered off into the woods?* I took a deep breath and tried to shake off my worry, but it gnawed inside me like a beaver chewing through wood.

When two women came down the trail toward us, we moved our sled to the side to let them pass. They looked like sisters—both in their late thirties and stocky, with rust-colored hair twisted up into buns. Their backpacks appeared empty, so I figured they had given up their quest and were heading back to town.

"Could we talk a moment?" Sadie asked them.

"Sure," one said. They stopped.

"Did you see a sled pulled by goats?"

"Yes, I did." She chuckled. "Only one on the trail."

"Was there a dark-haired girl with them? About eight-years-old?"

"Don't recall," she answered.

"How long would it take to reach them?"

"They're about six miles up by now. May not sound like much, but it's a steep grade of twists and turns and takes hours to climb. Might reach them by nightfall. All depends on where they camp. Are they your men?" the woman asked.

"No," Sadie said. "The little girl is their sister." She pointed to Viorene and me. "She considers one of the goats her pet and took off to save it."

"By herself?"

"That's what we fear."

"Oh, no," both women said. "Good luck," they said as they walked away.

A moment later, one of the women called back. "After we fill up our packs, we're hiking back to our camp. If you allow us to put our load on your sled, we'd help you pull."

"How long would it take you to get back from town?" Sadie asked.

"You don't understand," the woman said, coming toward us. "We're not going back to town. We're on a supply relay. We started with a full load, but as the elevation increased, we stashed some of our goods and carried what we could to our camp. We're back to retrieve more of our supplies. It's stored just around the bend. Your sled would come in handy and save all of us time."

Sadie glanced at Viorene and me. "Sounds good to me. Girls, what do you think?"

"Yes," Viorene answered.

"I'm in too," I told her.

"Great," the woman said, waving her sister over. "I'm Bertha. This is my twin, Betty."

As we introduced ourselves, I studied their faces and caught their differences. Betty had a thinner face, a missing side-tooth—only visible when she smiled—and a brown mole at the corner of her mouth. The shyer one of the two, her voice was soft and sweet. Not Bertha. She blurted out words, loud as a hog caller at a county fair.

Sadie guarded our sled, and Viorene and I followed the ladies to their stockpile.

"One ton of goods required," Bertha said. "The Mounted Police weigh it at the summit border. In the last five days, we've been up and back ten times. And, we're the lucky ones. Our camp has two mules. Any chance you girls could carry supplies on your backs? We got extra backpacks."

"Thought you were going to put them on our sled?" Viorene said.

"We are," Bertha said. "But if you carry some too, we might only have to make two more return trips, instead of three."

"No," Viorene said. "Can't chance affecting my posture. And, Aggie, you shouldn't either. We're both awful thin."

"Did you say posture? *Hee, haw,*" Bertha howled. She bent over, slapped her knee, and snorted out a laugh that reminded me of a cross between a squealing pig and a donkey.

I tried to refrain, but I chortled too.

Viorene glared at me.

"I'm sorry," I whispered to my sister. "It's just Bertha has a funny laugh."

Betty touched Viorene's shoulder. "She didn't mean any offense," she said, giggling. "But any amount you carry helps us. Even if it's a coffee tin."

"I suppose I could do that," Viorene huffed.

After a few trips back and forth from their hidden supply to Sadie, we loaded the sled. Betty and Bertha strapped on their stuffed-full backpacks. Then Bertha strapped one on to me. As I plodded through the mud, it seemed to weigh heavier with each step. Viorene carried the filled coffee tin, shifting it from hand to hand and appeared annoyed. But secretly, I would've traded places with her in a frog's leap.

When it was our turn to spell Betty and Bertha pulling the sled, they walked ahead and disappeared around the bend. I pulled off the pack, aimed for the grass, but it landed in mud.

My back ached something fierce.

Viorene looked at me. "You all right?"

"No," I said, stretching. "Weighs heavier than a cast-iron bell."

"We'll put it on the sled," Viorene said. "That's what I did with the coffee tin."

"There's no room."

Sadie lifted the backpack. "I'll carry it for a bit." After she strapped it on, she gripped the sled's rope at the front. I picked up the other one. Viorene stood behind me.

"One, two, three, *pull*," Sadie said.

The sled barely moved an inch.

"We're too small to do this," Viorene said in a disgusted tone. "They've weighed it down."

Sadie nodded. "Seems this didn't work out to our advantage, but we have to try. Instead of all of us pulling, why don't you girls push from behind?"

Sure enough, our pushing and Sadie pulling did move the sled, but at a banana-slug pace. And every few feet we had to rest.

Sadie took off the backpack. "I can't carry this and pull." She looked at me. "And, it's too heavy for you too. Either we find a spot on the sled or leave it behind."

I reached into the pack and pulled out a five-pound bag of salt and baking soda and yeast, and crammed them into every spare crevice on the sled.

"Don't know where I'm going to put the rest," I said.

Then without one word, Sadie grabbed the pack and lobbed it down a gulley, with half their supplies still inside.

I gasped and looked at Viorene.

"Time to get moving again," Sadie said, taking hold of the rope.

"Glad you did that," Viorene told her.

"Serves them right for overloading you like that," Sadie said. "You gotta learn to say no when it makes sense, Aggie."

Much as I didn't want to admit it, she was right. Mama called me a people-pleaser. Said it was a good trait, if not abused. Most cases, it worked against me because I found it hard to say no. Viorene was one too, but only if it worked to her benefit. Not Wilmina. She never shied away from saying no.

Up ahead, Betty and Bertha leaned against a boulder. We stopped when we reached them.

"Where's your backpack?" Bertha asked me.

I gulped and looked up at Sadie.

"Got too heavy," Sadie said. "We took out the supplies and stuffed them and the pack onto the sled."

I didn't like that she lied, but was learning real quick that with unknown people it was best to say what they wanted to hear. Otherwise, you might end up in a bigger mess.

Bertha nodded. "Might as well have a seat. Not going anywhere." She pointed to the corduroy bridge about a half-mile up—made of logs tied together by ropes—that spanned over a rocky river.

"A log shifted and a horse fell through," she said. "Now the wagon's stuck and caused a blockade."

"How far do you think we've traveled?" Sadie asked.

"About three miles. Our camp's another two, at the base of Devil's Hill. With this slow-moving line, it'll take us at least four hours to reach it. How you holding up with the sled?"

"Not good," Sadie said. "With the added weight, we can barely move it. Once the grade increases more, I doubt if we can do it at all."

"What we figured. There'll be a point where Betty and I can't either." She cleared her throat. "I was thinking. Aggie could come with us and look for her sister. You and Viorene stay with the sled. We'll come back early morning with my boys."

Viorene's mouth flew open. "Out here alone in the dark?" Her voice trembled. "There's wolves and bears out here."

"The darkness only lasts a few hours."

"No," Sadie said. "We're coming with you. Hide the sled."

"It'll be stolen."

"Your supplies weren't bothered before, were they?"

"No, they were hid," Bertha said. "But at the start of the trail, not such a treasure. Found three miles up? That makes them gold. Saves close to six hours of back and forth."

"Our mission isn't to guard supplies," Sadie said. "It's to find their little sister. And, I'm *not* being separated from these girls and we're not stopping until we get to a camp."

Bertha's furrowed brows and puckered lips told me she was about to blow. I interrupted. "Let's check the crowd at the bridge. Maybe Wilmina's there."

"Good idea." Sadie clutched onto Viorene's arm and pulled her along.

When we came back, Betty and Bertha hadn't budged one inch. "Take it she wasn't there," Bertha said.

"No," Sadie said. "Time to get this sled hidden."

Bertha frowned at Sadie, but nonetheless she and Betty got up. What choice did they have? Most of the supplies on the sled belonged to them.

We removed sacks and hid them in bushes to lighten the load and then pulled the sled behind a large bush, turned it on its side, and covered it with twigs. After I marked the hide-out locations in my journal, I tore out the page and handed it to Bertha.

She huffed and then stuffed the paper into her pocket. "Thanks for nothing," she said.

We reloaded our gunnysacks with some of the food that Viorene had packed and I carried the water jug too. And we each took a blanket, but were too tired to haul more. Bertha and Betty loaded up too.

"Hope our supplies don't get stolen," Bertha snapped. "Crowd's moving now."

Sadie whispered. "Let them walk ahead on their own, but keep them in view. We might need their help later."

The line moved at caterpillar pace and more than once halted for what seemed hours. By the time we reached Bertha and Betty's camp, my legs wobbled and I collapsed in tall scone-like snake grass. Viorene and Sadie did the same. Without warning, mosquitoes swarmed, buzzed our ears, and landed on our skin.

"Darn bugs," Sadie said, swatting her neck. "We forgot the netting on the sled." Sadie had packed a bolt along.

Bertha and Betty headed to a canvas tent beyond, one of many scattered here and there. When they returned, they offered a hot bowl of beans. "Come over to the campsite and dish some up," Bertha said. "We'll share our food, but we expect repayment from your supplies."

"Of course," Sadie said. "In fact, the sooner we find Wilmina, the more we can give you."

I could tell from Bertha's face that Sadie's offer pleased her.

"Good." She pointed. "You'll be sleeping in that tent. Moved my little ones in with me."

"Thank you," Sadie said. "Any chance you got mosquito netting? We'll replace it."

"Yards of it in the tent. Take what you need."

Viorene had fallen asleep in the grass. I shook her awake. "Come on. Mosquitoes are eating you for supper. Let's get you to bed."

Sadie and I held on to Viorene as she stumbled over to the tent. When we got inside, we saw that the ground was covered with pine branches. Sadie pulled up her skirt and stripped off three layers underneath it. "For our mattress," she said, sprawling the skirts over the branches. Viorene plopped down onto it and she was snoring as soon as she closed her eyes. After Sadie and I ate some deer jerky, we did the same.

Alaska State Library - Historical Collections

White Pass Trail
(Corduroy bridge over Skagway River, 1898)

*(Courtesy of Alaska State Library, Historical Collections,
Winter and Pond Trail of '98 Photo Collection
ASL-P21-07)*

Alaska State Library - Historical Collections

White Pass Trail
(Camp at foot of summit, Skagway trail, Alaska, 1898)

(Courtesy of Alaska State Library, Historical Collections,
Winter and Pond Trail of '98 Photo Collection
ASL-P21-10)

CHAPTER 8
WHITE PASS

AWAKENED BY GIGGLING children touching my face, I bolted upright. For a moment, I had forgotten where I was until I looked down and saw Viorene and Sadie fast asleep beside me.

"Shhh...," putting my finger over my mouth. I motioned the children to follow me. Soon as we crawled outside, it appeared we were the late-starters of the day.

The kids scurried away.

I went from tent to tent, shivering from the cold drizzle hitting me, as I looked for Wilmina. The wind howled too. When I saw Betty at a campfire and smelled sizzling bacon, my stomach growled. I hurried to her.

"What a soggy day," I said.

She smiled. "Have a seat, coffee, and bacon." She placed a canvas sheet over me. "To keep you dry and mosquito free. They come out on dreary days."

"Thank you." I reached for a tin plate. "Surprised you have a fire with all this moisture."

"We tent it with sticks and sprinkle in dry tinder—fluffed-up dry leaves, a bird's nest, or small pinecones—to light the fire. Prospectors taught us all types of tricks. They even brew beer out of pine needles. Said it keeps scurvy away."

"Never heard such a thing but good to know. We have lots of pine trees back home." I looked around. "Where's Bertha?"

"Left an hour ago with her two older sons to retrieve your sled. Took the mule."

"Why didn't you have the mule on your relay down, when we met you?"

"We tried it once and swore never again. Too hard to move an animal off the trail when a stream of people are coming at you. We had to turn around and hike with them until we got to a clearing. But with her sons along, they run ahead and scout the way."

"She must be awful tired."

"She's strong as a bear. I'm the one who has to rest, but I'll go tomorrow. Got at least five more trips before we can start the next leg."

As I ate, Betty explained how prospectors— sometimes called gold seekers, stampeders, and the experienced ones, sourdoughs—all traveled in relays. This camp, their first, would be one of many. After retrieving their stockpile at the base, they'll re-hide it near this camp, head up another five miles or so, and start the relay all over again.

"Sure seems hard," I said. "Where are your husband's?"

"Dead. Mine from a wagon accident. Bertha's didn't really die, just took off and never came back. But he's dead to her."

"You're doing this without men?"

"Yes. Iowa farming dried up from the drought, so we pooled our money for a new start."

I smiled at her, but knowing they were banking on something that would more than likely destroy their lives, sickened me. Sadie had told us all about it as we walked the trail.

She said the few who actually found gold were long gone—most of the claims had been dug dry. The new prospectors coming would either be sold false claims or gutted-out ones. By the time they realized their fate, they'd die from scurvy, get killed, or be so broken and penniless they'd lose their way. And most that traveled White Pass waited until winter for the mud to freeze, but conditions were harsh—snowfall so thick they trudged along blinded and bitter whistling winds that never eased up. And if they reached Lake Bennett, they'd camp until spring when the lake thawed, then build watercrafts to sail the five-hundred miles or so to the Klondike, over rapids so fierce it could take a life.

"Do you still have family back home?"

"Cousins. They tried to talk us out of coming, but Bertha was determined. We're trying to get as far up the trail as we can with our relays before the mud turns to slush. Then we'll hunker down until the trail hardens to ice. But we're hearing the trail's not so bad, and if the Mounties aren't guarding the summit, we might get lucky and make it to Lake Bennett and to the Klondike before winter hits."

"I hope that's the case." I put down my plate. "I better get Viorene and Sadie up. Thank you for the food."

"Bring them over. I'll fry up more bacon and beans."

When I told Sadie about Betty and Bertha, she shook her head.

"Shouldn't we try to stop them? You said the summit was a thousand-foot climb."

"Won't do any good. Once they've been struck by the fever, they have to see it through. They're strong women. Even if they don't strike gold, they'll carve out a life somehow, some way."

Sadie and Viorene followed me to Betty's campsite and plunked down in front of the fire. Sadie reached for a tin cup. "Coffee, thank goodness. The one thing I can't live without."

As Sadie and Viorene ate, Betty packed up three gunnysacks for each of us to carry.

"You and Bertha keep the sled and the rest of our supplies packed on it," Sadie said.

"Doesn't seem like a fair trade," Betty said.

"It's too heavy for us to pull."

"Stop back on your way down," Betty said. "We'll stock you up again."

"Will do. Give Bertha our best. And thank you both for all the hospitality. Sure appreciate you feeding us and letting us sleep in your tent."

Viorene and I thanked her too.

BACK ON THE TRAIL, the grade got steeper and narrower as we climbed, but still surrounded by trees and streams. Luckily, the drizzle let up, but the wind didn't.

Suddenly my leg cramped. "Ow, ow, ow," I moaned, limping to a fallen log. Sadie and Viorene sat next to me as I rubbed my thigh.

We watched a group of prospectors pass. I studied every one, figuring one might be Daddy coming back on a relay. And my, did we catch their attention. Or, should I say, Sadie did. One prospector even whistled through his teeth. I could see why— Sadie wasn't plain like the other women on the trail. Even without being gussied up, she had beauty, especially with her long wavy hair, red as a flaming fire. Thank goodness no one noticed Viorene, but who would with all the mud covering her face.

Sadie pulled out the water jug, took a swig, and handed it to Viorene, who gulped and gulped. Then my sister passed it to me.

"You didn't leave much," I said to her as I tapped the bottom of the jug.

"Don't squabble over water," Sadie said. "Streams all through here."

"I'll fill it now." I hobbled away, looking down into the gully.

Just then, another group of prospectors appeared, but instead of going up, they were coming down.

"Any of you see a sled with goats?" I asked.

No one answered, but one shabby-looking prospector smiled at me—showing his rotten teeth— then noticed Sadie and Viorene on the log and headed straight toward them.

His group continued on.

"Ain't you a looker," he said to Sadie as he approached.

I followed him but kept my distance.

Sadie stood and smiled. "Better keep moving. Your friends are leaving you behind."

"Want to know about goats?" he said.

"Have you seen them?"

"Tell you, if you give me a kiss."

Sadie frowned. "Never mind. We'll find them ourselves."

Viorene stood and reached for Sadie's hand, but the prospector grabbed Sadie's arm first, then he puckered up his lips and leaned toward her face.

"Stop it," she demanded. "Get out of here."

"One little peck ain't goin' to hurt you."

Viorene froze and gave me a panicked, get-over-here look.

When I got within reach, I pulled on the old man's coat.

He elbowed me in the chin.

As Sadie fought him off, Viorene pointed to a good-sized, jagged rock. It took both of us to lift it. We inched over and dropped it on his boot.

"Holy cow," he hollered as he released Sadie. "You broke my foot." He hopped around, cussing, trying to hold his broken foot.

Sadie pushed him and he landed on his butt.

"Run," she screamed.

After we grabbed our gunnysacks, the three of us scampered fast as rabbits chased by a wolf. I could tell Sadie was worried 'cause she kept looking over her shoulder. I looked too and sure was relieved when I saw the prospector shuffle away.

I stopped. "He's gone."

Viorene stood next to me trembling like a scared pup. I slipped my hand around hers. "We'll be fine. We should be coming to a camp any time."

At the next bend, we spotted tents.

"Look for women," Sadie said.

"Over there." I pointed to a thin woman with stringy gray hair and dressed in rags.

"She's a back-hiller," Sadie whispered. "Careful with your words." Sadie quickly explained that back-hill people lived like mountain men and didn't trust outsiders, but I also knew that it was a two-sided coin, recalling a conversation with Daddy.

On one of our trips to town someone whispered, "river people," like it was a disgraceful thing to be. When I came back to the boat all upset, Daddy explained that the world was made up of all types of people. "Most are hardworking folks," he had said, "just trying to survive." But he also added that there were judgmental people who might view themselves superior, which could cause caution and mistrust from the other side. I told him that I was proud to be a river person. He smiled and said that he was too. He then told me don't judge people by the way they look or live, but how they act.

AS WE NEARED the woman, she sneered at Sadie.

Sadie smiled. "Hello. We're looking for a sled pulled by goats."

"Why would the likes of you be interested in goats?" the woman said, revealing bare gums that used to possess teeth. "You one of those showgirls?"

"No."

"Liar."

"Please, it's important."

"Was here, but left. Now git out of my camp."

"When did they leave?" I asked.

She ignored me and walked away.

I looked at Sadie. "You think that prospector who tried to kiss you was from here?"

"Could be. Most back-hillers have rotten teeth."

I didn't question her, but in my finding that was a common trait of half the prospectors I'd seen. I prayed that wouldn't happen to Daddy. He was known for his perfect smile, same one as Viorene.

We rested on a log at the edge of the trail. When I got up to stretch my legs, I spotted three prospectors coming up the trail. I wished I had my binoculars, but they were left on the sled. I could see well enough that one of them had a walking cane and limped real bad. I rushed over to Sadie and Viorene.

"Get up. Prospectors are coming. One of them has a limp."

"What?" Sadie said. "Can't be back this soon."

She and Viorene followed me to a tree and peeked around it. "Might be coming back because he's injured. What'd we do?" I asked.

She looked side to side. "Head into the woods beyond that tent. We'll hide there."

"But we have to go through the camp to get there," Viorene said. "What if that woman sees us again?"

"Move," Sadie said, pushing Viorene forward.

I followed, but truthfully had the same concern as my sister.

No sooner had we slumped down behind a tree stump, we heard voices.

"Are they coming this way?" Viorene whispered.

"Can't tell."

"I knew we shouldn't have come in here," she said.

Sadie put her finger to her lips for us to hush.

CHAPTER 9
WHITE PASS

IN THE WOODS, we hid, scrunched together behind a stump. First my leg cramped up again, then my foot and bottom. Sadie and Viorene complained of the same thing, so we took turns standing up and stretching. On my next turn, I crept over to a moss-covered tree trunk, crouched behind it, and studied the camp. Then I hurried back to Sadie and Viorene.

I pointed to the right. "Prospectors are sitting at campfires. The opposite side appears open, but it's a longer route. Clear around the edge of the camp."

Sadie stood and brushed pine needles off her skirt. "Aggie, lead the way."

"It's too dangerous," Viorene said. "We should wait until dark."

"We can't afford to lose more time," Sadie said. She grabbed Viorene's hand and pulled her along.

When we got to a bush, Sadie and Viorene squatted behind it. I scurried over to a tree and surveyed, then signaled for them to come ahead. Doing this, we made it halfway around the camp without a hitch. Until I stepped on a branch. It cracked and riled five floppy-eared hound dogs tied to a post.

They jumped up and down and howled and howled and howled.

"H*owl...Howl...Howl.*"

One set off the other.

I mouthed to Sadie and Viorene. "W*ait,*" then ducked behind a tree.

A man came out of a tent—probably the dogs' owner—and looked around.

"What is it, Buck?" another man said as he poked his head out of the same tent.

"Must be a squirrel or a rabbit," the first man said. "Hounds bark at anythin' that moves."

Soon as he turned his back, Sadie and Viorene rushed over to me, but the tree wasn't wide enough to conceal all three of us. The dogs started up again.

Sadie frowned. "I'm tired of this game. Let's just walk out of here."

Viorene's eyes widened. "What if we're seen?"

"What're they going to do?" Sadie said. "Eat us for supper?"

"Hey," the dogs' owner hollered, coming toward us. "What you doin' over there?"

He had the same sloppy appearance as the woman we'd met earlier—lanky build, gnarled unkempt hair, missing teeth, and patched clothes.

"Sorry," Sadie said. "Got turned around in your camp. We'll be on our way."

We didn't get but five steps when the ornery woman saw us. She hustled over. "Thought you left. Bet you've been thievin' our tents." She glanced at the man. "Can't trust these no-good showgirls."

"I'm done with this conversation," Sadie said. "Girls, come on."

"Not so fast," the man said, seizing Sadie's arm. "Need to check your sacks."

Sadie threw her gunnysack at the man's feet. "Hurry up, so we can be on our way." Viorene and I dropped our sacks on the ground too.

"Ain't the way our camp works," the woman piped up. "Need everyone to identify the goods."

In the center of the camp stood a make-shift bell tower. Soon as the hag rang the bell, people sauntered over and circled around. Mostly men, but some women and kids too.

"Thieves," the woman spouted. She dumped our belongings—uneaten sandwiches, deer jerky, mosquito netting, bootlaces, and gloves. "Empty your pockets too."

I reached into my pocket and clasped my five-dollar coin, the one I earned from working on the fish traps with Daddy. I struggled with letting it go. I glanced at Sadie. She nodded and tossed a handful of dollars on the ground. I threw my coin down too.

"What's hangin' from that chain?" the old woman said.

She grabbed for my pocket watch.

"No." I jumped back. "That belongs to my father. I'm *not* giving it up."

The crone paused. "Got spunk, give you that. Keep it. Got no need for it anyway."

"I see, I see," a young girl announced. "A five-dollar gold piece." She picked it up and folded her fingers around it. "Mine."

"That's Aggie's," Viorene said, outraged. "She worked hard for that. Give it back."

The young girl stared at Viorene, then at me. Without a word she handed me the gold piece. I tried to say thank you, but she quickly turned and walked away.

After some of the others picked through our things, leaving nothing but a jug of water and a bootlace, Sadie pulled us along through the camp. No one stopped us. Not even the cantankerous woman.

At the trail, we took off and sprinted for what seemed like miles. When we stopped, my heart thumped so hard it ached to breathe. My throat had gotten so raw I could barely talk.

"Could've been worse," Sadie said in a hoarse voice. "Back-hill people live by a different code. Be thankful one of them didn't want me for a wife. Or you girls for future brides."

"What?" Viorene said. "You mean we're in danger up here?"

"Afraid so. I should've thought this out better and brought men along."

"You tried," I said, "but Jimmy said no."

She puckered her lips. "Don't get me started on that. Probably would've been more of a hindrance."

Huffing and puffing, we climbed along the slippery trail. With ten-foot high boulders on one side and drop-off cliffs, hundreds of feet down, on the other, we rested where we stood.

Viorene touched Sadie's arm. "I'm afraid to go into another camp. What if it's like the last one?"

"Understand your concern, but we have to take that chance. Only way to find your sister."

I spoke up. "Besides, most up here are prospectors. Lots of them families."

"True," Sadie said. "It was just bad luck to wander into a back-hill camp."

"Twice," Viorene added. "We went into it twice."

AS THE TRAIL descended into a valley, I spotted another camp near a creek with only a handful of canvas tents, all a good distance apart. Single-file, I led Sadie and Viorene through tall, insect-filled wet grass that soaked our clothes up to our knees. Sadie lifted her skirts and trudged through it, but got as wet as Viorene and me.

"This is miserable," Sadie said, spitting out bugs and swatting them away from her face.

"Campfire this way," I said, following a stomped-down path.

I stopped mid-step, spun around, and looked at Sadie and Viorene. "GOATS!"

"Where?" Viorene squealed.

I pointed, "By that tent," and then raced ahead.

"Wilmina. Billy. Jake. Are you here?" I yelled, running into the camp.

Jake poked his head out of a tent and groaned. "Not more of you," he said as he crawled out.

Billy came out from behind the tent.

"Is Wilmina with you?"

Before he could answer, Wilmina appeared holding a handful of hay.

I darted to my sister, flung my arms around her, and rocked back and forth.

Viorene ran to us, gushing tears. "How could you run off like that?"

"I had to. For Hillard."

"We discovered her after three miles," Jake said. "She was curled up on the wagon under a tarp. I didn't plan on returning with her any time soon."

"I was goin' to bring her back," Billy said. "Today, in fact."

Jake looked hard at Billy. "Did you forget I hired you for a job?"

"I was coming back."

"That maneuver would've cost us at least three days."

Sadie sat down next to the fire. "Stop bickering. We're here to take her. Just thankful you stopped early."

"Had to," Jake said, now sitting across from Sadie. "Next grade is up Porcupine Hill. Have to leave the wagon behind, load up our sled, and pack the rest on our backs and the horses. Prospectors are paying good money for us to transport their goods."

"After hiking this trail, I see why they hired you," Sadie said. She motioned to the pot on the fire. "Any coffee left? Need food and water too. We're starved."

"I'll get cups and plates," Billy said.

I sat next to Sadie and pulled Wilmina down between Viorene and me.

"You sure caused a scare," I scolded. "Don't know what we would've done if we hadn't found you."

She bit her lip. "I'm sorry."

Sadie spoke up. "If you were my kid, I'd take a willow stick to you."

Wilmina gasped.

What Sadie didn't understand was that ever since Mama died, Wilmina got frozen in time, and sometimes acted younger than eight.

"No punishment this time," I added. "Just glad you're safe. But don't ever pull anything like that again."

Billy handed everyone cups, lifted the coffeepot, and filled them. "Got grits and hot beans in that kettle," he said, pointing to a pot sitting in the dirt. He set the plates on the ground next to it. "Can you serve yourselves? I need to pack."

"That's right," Jake said. "Didn't hire you to play hostess. I'll feed the animals." He stood and went over to an improvised goat pen made of wire and tree limbs.

After we ate, my sisters and I gathered the dirty plates and carried them to a washtub.

"Psst, Aggie," Billy whispered. "Come here,"

"Be right back," I told my sisters and headed over to Billy by the sled.

"Been showin' your father's picture around," he said. "A prospector comin' down from above was pretty certain he saw your dad at Horse Bridge Camp. Said he's scruffier lookin'."

"Where's that?"

"At least two days up, but he's gotta be doing relays. Didn't sound like he had a sled."

Sadie startled me when she spoke behind me. "What's going on?"

I turned around. "A prospector spotted my father two days from here."

"Nothing you can do about it," she said. "Your priority is getting your sisters back to the boat."

"Couldn't you take them?"

"No," she said firmly. "Not leaving any of you girls up here."

"I'd be fine."

"After what happened on the way up? No, we're safer in numbers."

"She's right," Billy said. "Besides, I can find him good as you."

I nodded, but felt like I'd been punched in the gut. I also knew Sadie's confidence had been jarred and she didn't feel safe on the mountain. If only I could convince her she'd be fine, so she'd let me go with Billy.

"Somethin' else, real important, you need to know," Billy said.

Before he could continue, Jake walked up. "I sold the baby and the mother," he blurted out.

"What?" Sadie and I said at the same time, turning to Jake.

"To a prospector name McGuire going down the trail," Jake said. "A stowaway on the *Irene*. That makes her part of my load." He sneered at me. "You said that very thing to me about the baby. Same applies to the mother."

"Who told you about Inga?" I said.

He pointed to Wilmina. "Paid off having her along after all."

"Wilmina," Viorene said. "How could you?"

"Uhh...," she mumbled. "I didn't mean to."

Billy interrupted. "She's tellin' the truth. Jake overheard us talkin' about Inga's hair. How it reminded us of yellow poppies. We didn't know he was behind us."

"Soon as I heard she was as pretty as Viorene, I knew I had a treasure," Jake said smugly. "Had two prospectors bidding. Got eighty dollars for her. He's on his way to the *Irene* to collect her."

"You louse." Sadie said, flipping her coffee toward him.

He jumped back, the hot brew landed at his feet.

"How long ago did that prospector leave?" Sadie demanded.

"Can't say."

"You mean, you won't." She glanced at Billy. "Do you know?"

Billy nodded. "Earlier, this morning. Five or six hours ago."

Wilmina stomped over to Jake. "You promised you'd keep what I said a secret." She turned to me, tears in her eyes. "Honest, Aggie, he promised." She gulped in air, and then her lisp set in. "He as*th*ked more about Inga last night while we fed the goats. S*th*aid I hurt his feelings. A true friend would tell him the truth. Even told me I could have Hillard if I s*th*owed good faith."

I glared at Jake. "Pretty low of you to trick a little girl."

He shrugged.

"You're slimier than a slug," Sadie said. She turned to Billy. "Hope you got paid up front, because you're escorting us down to Bertha and Betty's camp. Don't care if you come back here or not."

THE NEXT MORNING, Sadie softened a bit.

"If circumstances were different," she said to me, "I'd let you go and look for your father, but I have to think of your sisters' safety first. If something happened to me, they'd be on their own. It's too dangerous up here for young girls."

"I understand." Truthfully, I wished I didn't, but I knew my sisters had to come first. Even before Daddy. That's the way my parents would've viewed it.

"But I will agree to have Billy stay behind," Sadie said. "He can start his search for your father today."

"That would make me feel better."

"We'll just have to be cautious when we pass the back-hiller camp," she said.

"Okay, but we should hide your hair so not to draw attention from other prospectors." I took off my captain's hat and handed it to her.

She shook her head. "You need it."

"No one's going to give me a second glance. I'm a buck-toothed kid. Not pick of the litter."

"Don't think that way," she scolded. "You're cute as can be. In your own way."

Truth, I didn't care how I looked. I just wanted to be a sea captain, wearing overalls covered in grease. Only girly fact about me—choosing not to smell. Every day I washed up, brushed my teeth, and chewed wild mint for my breath.

I handed her the hat again. "Please take it."

After Sadie tucked every inch of her hair under the hat, she smeared dirt all over her face. Viorene copied Sadie, then darkened her front teeth with gooey mud. Wilmina and I left our faces and teeth clean.

Billy packed us food and a jug of water. Jake made himself scarce.

"Thank you again," I told Billy as I lifted the gunnysack.

"I'll find him," he said, "and bring him back."

I smiled and nodded. "Thank you for that."

I knew Billy had made a tall pledge. First, he had to find Daddy. Then convince him to come back. Billy was a good talker, but to persuade Daddy because of a photo? I wasn't sure. I craved with all my heart to be going with Billy. I shook it off. Can't think about wish-I-coulds now. My first priority—my sisters. To get them and Sadie safely back to town.

"Time to go," Sadie called out. "Where's Wilmina?"

"With the goats," I said. "I'll get her."

Alaska State Library - Historical Collections

White Pass Trail
(Men and mules packing hay bales)
(Note the long trail of people behind them)

**(Courtesy of Alaska State Library, Historical Collections,
Case and Draper Photo Collection, ca. 1898-1920,
ASL-P39-0849)**

White Pass Trail
(Overall view of men and animals on snowy trail)

*(Courtesy of Alaska State Library, Historical Collections,
Case and Draper Photo Collection, ca. 1898-1920,
ASL-P39-0851)*

CHAPTER 10
WHITE PASS

WE GOT past the back-hillers' camp without a hitch, but not before I had scouted it out. Now farther down the trail, we finally took a breather and slowed to a reasonable pace. It was a lot easier going down than it had been going up.

"We should've brought Hillard," Wilmina repeated.

Sadie jerked her to a stop. "That goat's welfare is the least of our problems. Start thinking of others. Instead of yourself."

Wilmina wiggled out of Sadie's grip and dashed ahead.

I hurried to her and yanked her arm. "Don't even think about running off." I glanced back at Sadie and Viorene and could tell by their faces they were too frustrated to listen to anymore of Wilmina's jabber about the goat.

When we reached Bertha and Betty's camp, I spotted Bertha sitting at their campfire. I grabbed Wilmina's hand and treaded us through the tall grass. "Hello, Bertha," I hollered.

She looked up. "Is this your missing sister?" she asked excitedly.

"Yes. Right where expected. With the goats."

Sadie and Viorene walked up. Bertha gawked.

"What happened to you?" she said. "Looks like you've been dragged through the mud."

"Had to disguise ourselves," Viorene offered. "A prospector made advances to Sadie and Aggie dropped a huge rock on his foot."

I looked at Viorene and shook my head, but her not admitting her part with the rock didn't surprise me. That would've meant she had acted un-lady-like, and to her proper behavior ranked high up on her list. She'd never come clean about it if she didn't have to.

Bertha interjected. "Good for you, Aggie. Survival puts people at odds. Speaking of survival, I wanted to thank all of you for giving us your sled. The whole camp was excited when they heard."

She explained that the camp worked like a wagon train, same as the one she and Betty took from Iowa to come west. They traveled together and shared supplies. Having a sled hooked to a mule meant they could relay more from their stockpiles.

"There's a bigger concern than the prospector," Sadie said. "Might affect you folks." After Sadie told Bertha about the back-hill people, Bertha frowned.

"Sorry for your mishaps, but it's good to know about those folks. Sounds like the very spot we'll be camping on our next relay."

Sadie nodded. "That's what I figured."

"I'd feel better if you had a man escorting you back," Bertha said. "Let me see if Cyrus has left."

A moment later, she returned with Betty. "No time for chitchat or goodbyes," Bertha said. "Cyrus left about half-hour ago. If you hurry, you could catch him. Should be the only one with a mule pulling a sled." She handed me my binoculars. "Found these on the sled. Thought you'd like them back."

"Appreciate that," I told her.

"If you ever make it back to Skagway," Sadie told them. "Look me up."

WE RACED DOWN the trail at a record pace.

"There he is," I said. "Cyrus, Cyrus! Wait."

He stopped and turned around.

"We're friends of Bertha and Betty."

Sadie and my sisters trotted up behind me.

"Are you the sled people?" he said.

"That's us."

"Sure is a blessing to have it."

Wearing overalls, a green-plaid shirt, and a straw hat, Cyrus looked more like a farmer than a prospector. He appeared well-fed, clean, and had his long brown beard trimmed. I figured he had to have a wife.

As we walked, he told his whole story. He and his family of six came from Kentucky, searching for the gold-rush dream.

"Let me spell you." I took the mule's reins and walked up front. Wilmina stepped along on the other side and stroked the mule's nose.

"Is a mule a donkey?" she asked Cyrus.

"It's an offspring of a donkey and a female horse. And not as big, but more patient, sure-footed, and smarter. But you have to watch their legs."

"Why's that?" she asked, looking down at its hooves.

"They can kick from any direction, even sideways."

"Oh," she said.

"Wilmina," Viorene called out. "Better come back here and walk with me."

"All right," she said.

"Good." Sadie chuckled. "Last thing we need is you getting attached to a mule."

A crowd of prospectors approached. I spotted a clearing ahead and pulled the mule toward it. I scoured the group as they passed. One of the men had the same build as our bad encounter and used a walking stick as he limped along. Luckily, Wilmina and Viorene blocked Sadie from view. Not me, in front, for all to see.

Cyrus, behind me, acknowledged the group. "Howdy," he said.

Some responded with hello.

I had lowered my head, but as the tail of the group passed, I glanced up. As I did, the limping prospector locked eyes on my face. I jerked my head down again.

"Hold on." The prospector grabbed my arm.

Cyrus stepped up to my side. "Let go of her."

"Got attacked by girls on the way down. Similar appearance to her."

"Can't be," Cyrus said. "This is my wife and kids. The first time we've traveled down this trail."

"Don't believe you. Let me see your woman's hair."

"Told you to release my daughter," Cyrus said.

Soon as his grip loosened, I yanked my arm away and ran to the other side of the mule.

"Now git," Cyrus said, watching the prospector hobble away.

But as he reached the mule's butt, he started around it, and like a miracle from heaven, that blessed animal kicked sideways at the prospector. Right on his shin.

Sadie and my sisters raced to the front.

The prospector stumbled. Swear words flew out of his mouth. The other prospectors hooted and hollered so loud it stirred up the mule again. Out came another sideways kick, hitting the man harder. He fell to the ground, scrambling out of the mule's reach.

Cyrus walked over to the man. "Best you get moving," he said sternly. "You're riling my animal."

Two prospectors came over, chortling as they helped the man stand.

"That was close," I said, relieved. "We had a run-in with him earlier."

Cyrus smiled. "This old molly can sense trouble. She's gotten me out of more than one fix."

"What're you going to do if you run into him on your way back up?"

"That scrawny old prospector don't worry me none. This mule has a good bite too."

Cyrus didn't seem worried, but I was. What if that prospector put the puzzle together and came after us? All the way to town? Who knows what he'd want—money, or worse, revenge for breaking his foot?

After we helped Cyrus load the sled at the same stockpile location where we had met Bertha and Betty, we parted ways.

"All the best to you," Sadie said. "And, thank you again. Tell Bertha and Betty the same."

"Will do. If we ever meet again, I'll buy you girls a fancy meal. Expect to be rich someday."

I watched until he disappeared around the bend. I churned with sadness, partly from knowing the hardships he and the others would be facing and for not staying behind to search for Daddy. But when Skagway came in view, relief washed over me to be off that mountain. Two days climbing the trail, pulling a sled, and about eight hours to get down, tuckered me out. Every bit of me worn through.

"Warm food, a hot bath, and a nap," Sadie said. "Best medicine for all of us."

"I agree with that," I said, "but shouldn't we get back to the boat, to check on Inga?"

Sadie looked at me firmly. "Not alone."

Soon as we entered the music hall, Lillie Mae rushed over and gathered us into a hug. "Thank goodness you're all safe."

"These kids need food and rest," Sadie said.

Lillie Mae stared at Sadie. "You look close to collapse."

"I am, but I have one more thing to do." She hurried to the theater.

Lillie Mae escorted us to the kitchen and dished up plates of baked chicken, mashed potatoes, gravy, and green beans. I scooped my food in so fast that I got the hiccups, but I kept on eating.

Sadie entered the kitchen with two men, who had guns in the holsters strapped to their waist.

"Kids, this is Willie and Sam. They're going to the *Irene* to check things out. You stay here."

Both men, about thirty, reminded me of cowboys: plaid shirts and trimmed light-brown hair and beards. Willie, the taller one, even had a handlebar moustache that curled up at the ends. Sam wore a cowboy hat with a red feather in its band.

"If the dinghy's still at the dock," I said. "I could row you to the boat."

"No," Sadie said. "You're exhausted."

"Feel better, since I ate."

Willie interrupted. "Actually, her help would be appreciated. I'm not good with watercrafts. Sam either."

"You sure, Aggie?" Sadie asked. "I'm so tired, once I sit down, doubt I'll be able to get up again."

"I can do it," I reassured.

AS I ROWED, I tried to stroke quietly, but every time I pulled on the oars, it sounded like splashing beaver tails. When we got to the *Irene*, there was no ladder to climb.

I cupped my hands together and called out, "Captain Murphy."

A moment later, he peered over the stern's taffrail. "Aggie-girl, ye're all right," he said. "And...,"

"Everyone's safe, we found Wilmina."

He sighed. "Been worried sick. Who are these men with ye?"

"Friends of Sadie."

"Wait on." He pushed the ladder overboard and it bounced against the hull as it plummeted down. Then, he turned on the winch and lowered the pulley. After I hooked the dinghy to it, the men and I climbed aboard.

He hugged me. "Grand news about ye sister, but now another tailspin is brewin'. A serious one."

"We know. Jake sold Inga and the baby."

"Aye," he said. "When I saw a prospector rowin' over in such a hurry, I pulled up the pulley and ladder so he couldn't come aboard. Right off, he was wavin' a paper. Makin' demands, tellin' me he paid good money, and to turn 'em over. When I told him

I didn't know what he was talkin' about, he said he'd be back with others. And not on friendly terms."

CHAPTER 11
SKAGWAY

THE CAPTAIN TURNED to the two men. "Got any ideas on how to handle the hooligan?"

Willie twisted the end of his moustache. "Hmm...," he repeated, winding his moustache tighter and tighter. We all watched in fascination. Even Sam. When he let go of it, it sprung like a rubber band.

"Money," Willie said. "Pay off the prospector."

"He still might want to see her," Sam said. "Is she pretty?"

"Aye. And yellow hair."

"Best to get her off this boat and deny she ever existed," Sam said, "but we need to move quick."

As Inga changed into a pair of my overalls and stuffed her hair under my captain's hat, I wrapped Catrine in a blanket.

"Should be safe with Sadie and Lillie Mae, until we figure out a permanent plan," I told her.

She smiled at me sadly. "I'm sorry for the trouble."

"Not your fault."

Soon as Inga stepped out of the hatch with the baby, all eyes were fixed on her.

"Yep, he's going to want to keep her," Willie said. "Even if you paid the man, there's a good chance that he'd double cross. Let's get moving."

Willie placed Catrine inside his shirt and Inga and Sam climbed down the ladder to the dinghy. As they stood in the dinghy, Willie slowly climbed down one-handed, the other braced against the baby.

"Precious cargo," the captain said as we watched.

With Sam's assistance, Willie stepped into the dinghy, lifted Catrine out of his shirt and handed her to Inga. Then both men quickly climbed back up to the boat. The plan was for them to stay with the captain on the *Irene* and for me to get Inga and Catrine to the music hall.

When we got to town, I walked in front of Inga and went from side to side, shielding her from view whenever we passed a saloon. Soon as we arrived at the music hall, we rushed through the side door. Lillie Mae was sitting at the kitchen table. She jumped up when she saw us.

"We were worried sick," she said. "Come with me." We followed her to Sadie's dressing room. Before we could knock, the door flew open.

"Thank goodness." Sadie said, wrapping her arms around me. She looked at Lillie Mae. "Take Inga and the baby to the room behind the stage." Soon as they departed, Sadie pulled me down to her sofa. "Talk."

I babbled on so fast she made me slow down and repeat some of what I had said.

"That old geezer has wits," she said, referring to Captain Murphy. "Guess he's not so bad after all."

"Sam and Willie advised us to say that Inga never existed," I added.

"Might be safer for *all* of you to stay here, until you leave port," she said. "We could masquerade you as singers or other acts."

"What?"

"Entertainers are protected. It's a code of ethics. Even scoundrels abide. I wouldn't be surprised if you could juggle balls or throw knives."

"No. I do better disguised as a boy. Besides, someone needs to stay on the boat with the captain."

"Suppose that's true," she said. "We do need a go-between. But I insist you take a short nap."

"I am tired, but if I lie down now, I won't wake up until morning. I have to get back to the boat and let the captain know we got here safely."

"Let's go see your sisters first," Sadie said, escorting me to the door.

After I told them that they had to stay at the music hall, they both fussed.

"I don't want to stay here," Viorene said.

"Me, neither," Wilmina added.

"You don't have a choice," I said. "With that prospector looking for Inga, you're safer here. Especially you, Viorene. You might be mistaken for her."

"Oh," she gasped. "I never thought of that."

"Wilmina, you observe better than anyone. You'll be needed for that."

"I can do that," she said. "I'll keep them safe."

"I know you will. I love you both. I'll check in whenever I can."

Sadie followed me outside. "Don't barter with that prospector. If you mention money, he'll know Inga's real. You have to convince him Jake's a swindler and no friend of yours."

"But won't it put Billy in danger too?"

"Could. We just have to hope they don't meet up again."

When I got to the boat and told the captain Sadie's plan, he shook his head.

"Singers? Who in their right mind is goin' to believe that? You ain't doin' that, are ye?"

"No, but it might keep them safe."

"Blimey," he said. "First, it was haulin' the goats. Then a little baby. Now this. Never once could I've conjured up such things." He stomped around a bit, then said. "So all of 'em are goin' to sing?"

"Don't know. Viorene can hold a tune, but I'd be surprised if they convince her to do it. Not sure of Inga's voice, but Sadie said there's all types of acts. Some walk across in costumes, others dance. Then there's those who do acrobatics, like tumbling and twirling a stick on fire."

BY MID MORNING, I had already rowed Sam and Willie to the dock and finished all my boat chores. While the captain and I visited in the pilothouse, I kept watch with my binoculars on all the watercraft. When I spotted a raft coming toward our boat, I jumped up and focused the lenses.

"I count three men," I said. "The one rowing is the raft owner. There's a scraggly prospector and a cleaned-up one. Sure wish Sam and Willie hadn't left. What're we going to do?"

"Settle down," the captain said. I followed him outside to the taffrail. "Let me do the talkin'."

When the raft reached our boat, the clean-cut prospector yelled up for us to lower the ladder or he'd shoot a hole in our hull. Before the captain got a chance to say yes or no, *bang*—a shot went off, but it only grazed the boat.

"What nonsense is this?" the captain said to the prospectors, looking down at them.

The first prospector hollered at the scraggly man next to him. "Told you to wait." He looked up at the captain again. "Lower the ladder."

The captain turned to me. "Have to let 'em aboard. Go below and hide all the baby things."

In the galley, I stacked empty milk bottles into a basket, covered them with a blanket, and pushed it under my bed. Then, I picked up Wilmina's doll and Inga's dress and ribbons, and shoved them into the cookstove oven. No sooner had I closed the oven door when I heard the captain hollering for me from the hatch.

"Aggie, get up here."

I quickly climbed the stairs. Soon as I stepped onto the deck, I did what I normally didn't do—I smiled so big that my wide-gapped, bucked teeth must've looked like a beaver ready to chew on a log.

Only two men had come aboard—a scraggly prospector and the clean-cut one who I guessed was McGuire, the man who had bought Inga and Catrine from Jake.

"Is that your bride-to-be?" the scraggly prospector said, chuckling. "Appears you've been fleeced. Sure you don't want your money back?"

"Leave her be," the captain snapped. "She's me ten-year-old granddaughter."

Being so tall for my age—five-foot-five—I was shocked the captain said ten.

The clean-cut man, McGuire, who seemed to be the leader, walked over to me and looked me up and down, as if he was buying a prized mule. I stared at him square-on. I guessed him to be about my daddy's age, early thirties, and better kept than most prospectors: trimmed medium-brown hair, no beard, and an agreeable face. Even smelled like lavender soap. I figured he must've cleaned up and shaved to come out here.

"If this is her, I sure got took," he said. "She's nothing but a kid. Gangly too."

Others might've been offended by the rude remarks. Not me. For the first time in my life, I was thankful for my gopher smile.

"I'm still gonna search this boat," McGuire said.

"Won't do no good," the captain said. "We got nothin' to do with any of this. We're just a transport boat."

"Juneau one of your stops?"

"Might be."

"What do you charge?"

"Twenty a piece," the captain said. "One way."

"A bit steep," the man said.

The captain shrugged.

"How soon you leaving?"

"What makes ye think I'd want the likes of ye on me boat?"

"Listen, old man," McGuire said. "I don't believe one word out of your mouth. Got papers saying I'm entitled to a blonde-haired girl and a baby from this boat." He grabbed my arm. "I could claim this one, right now on the spot and sell her as a maid."

"Take ye hands off her," the captain demanded.

The prospector released my arm. "Got no interest in her, but I do in a ride. So I'd advise you keep your wits." The men headed to the hatch and disappeared down the stairs.

"Should I follow them?" I said to the captain.

"Nothin' we can do at this point. Best to keep our distance."

When they reappeared, I saw two jars of salmon stuffed in their coat pockets. The captain saw it too and shook his head. "Let it go," he whispered. He hobbled toward the men. "If ye want a ride, be back here in two days. Headin' out by five a.m."

"Good," the prospector said, then he and the scraggly one climbed down to the raft.

"I can't believe you're willing to transport them."

"Have to go to Juneau anyway. Noticed a leak in a piston, need to get it fixed. Willie said the closest blacksmith is in Juneau."

"I don't trust those men," I said. "What if they try to steal the *Irene* or rob us?"

"Have to take the chance. Sooner they're out of these parts, the safer fer everyone."

CHAPTER 12
SKAGWAY

NEEDING TO GET a message to Sadie forced me to town. I waited until mid-afternoon, then hurried along the planked walk, looking side to side. I spotted McGuire coming out of the general store. I crossed the street and pretended not to see him, but I could feel his eyes watching me. Can't let him see me going to the music hall, I thought.

I walked into the stable, saw no one inside, and ran into the first empty stall. I closed the stall door and crouched behind two stacked bundles of hay.

The horse in the next compartment whinnied.

A moment later, someone walked in, then went from stall to stall. When they got close to me, the horse whinnied again. My heart throbbed clear up to my throat.

The heavy boot steps continued to the end of the stalls, turned around, and headed back.

My heart raced even faster.

"Missy. Know you're in here. Just want to talk."

I wanted to yell for him to go away. Instead, I froze. Goose bumps popped up all over my arms.

"It's either now or on the boat," he said. "Might be better to face me now."

Mama used to say I had good intuition, trust my gut. It was saying stay put and not make a peep.

After a long silence, I heard the footsteps leave. I still didn't move until the stable grew silent. Then, I rushed to a wall, looked through a crevice, and saw a man walking up the street. I could tell by his clothes and hair that he was the same one who came to the boat.

After my shaking stopped, I dashed to the stable's open door. Once outside, my fear glued me against the wall. I needed to dart across to the music hall in the middle of the block, but I couldn't move. *What if he sees me?* I looked up and down the street again. No one in sight. I took a deep breath and rushed across to an alley between two buildings barely wide enough for me to walk through. Behind the buildings, a dirt road passed the back of the music hall. At the rear door, I jiggled the locked handle and knocked and knocked.

Sadie opened the door.

"Aggie!" she said in a surprised tone.

I rushed past her, bent over, and sucked in air.

"What's wrong?" she said, holding my shoulders.

"Followed," I said, gasping, "by the prospector. I hid in the stable until he left."

Sadie guided me to the kitchen table, pulled out a wooden chair next to Lillie Mae, and told me to sit.

I told them about McGuire coming to the boat, about his threats, and how the captain agreed to transport him to Juneau. And what he said when he followed me into the stable.

Sadie looked at Lillie Mae and shook her head.

"He sounds determined, but the captain's right. Best course is to get him out of town."

Lillie Mae stood, "I'll get your sisters."

As I ate, my sisters sat with me. "This chicken and dumplings are sure good. Hope I can take some to the captain."

"I'll pour them into a carrying pot for him," Viorene said, going over to the cookstove. "Gertie baked pies too. I'll pack one for you to take."

"Is Gertie a showgirl?"

"No, she's the cook. Keeps food warmed on the stove all day. Inga and I have been helping her."

"Not me," Wilmina piped up. "I'm painting stage scenes of the sky. It's for Inga and Viorene's act."

"Act," I said, choking back a mouthful of dumplings.

Viorene sighed. "I said no. Lots of good that did. Sadie said two similar girls was the only way to truly camouflage Inga."

"Etta and Elke, the Golden Dutch Girls," Wilmina said. "Sadie's having costumes made. They're to have their hair braided and rolled above each ear."

"Is that right?" I tried to mask my amusement, but I know my face showed it. "Which one are you?" I asked Viorene.

"Don't know and don't care. How much longer do we have to stay here?"

"Not sure."

When Sadie returned with Lillie Mae, they sat at the kitchen table with us.

"How soon do you leave for Juneau?" Sadie asked me.

"Tomorrow."

Viorene's mouth flew open. "Juneau?" She stared at me. "You never said anything about leaving."

"Didn't want to worry you, but we're transporting that prospector, and getting an engine part fixed. Should be back by the end of the week."

"What if something happens? We could be stuck here for life."

Wilmina gasped. "No," she said. "We need to go with you."

Lillie Mae reached across the table and squeezed Wilmina's hand. "This is the safest place for you now. They'll only be gone a week. When they return, you'll be able to go back to the boat."

"Then I don't see the point of practicing for an act," Viorene said matter-of-factly.

"Sorry," Sadie said, "but we already told the owner. He plans to check on progress daily. You must've seen him—about forty, no facial hair, always in a gray suit. A distinguished looking businessman."

Viorene nodded. "I thought he was a customer."

"He's proud of this music hall, and especially excited to have blonde girls performing. Plans to have posters made up."

"He'll just have to be disappointed," she said.

"It would put Lillie Mae and me on the spot if you didn't perform. And remember Inga is also wanted by that saloon owner in Juneau who claimed her as his mail-order bride."

Viorene rolled her eyes and sighed.

"Aggie," Sadie said, "I arranged for the stable owner to transport you to the wharf. I hear the wagon now." She opened the back door. I hugged my sisters and walked out with Sadie and Lillie Mae. Sadie hugged me, kissed my cheek, and helped me into the rear of the wagon. Then she handed me the carrying pot of food.

"Be safe," Lillie Mae said, setting the pie next to me.

"See you and the old geezer in a week or so," Sadie said. She covered me with a blanket, then hit the back of the wagon. The driver snapped the reins and the wagon slowly bounced away.

Once I got into the dinghy, I rowed fast as I could to the *Irene*. The captain must've seen me coming. He had a bucket hanging from the pulley and he stood at the taffrail as I approached the boat.

"Hope ye brought food."

"Yes, and a blackberry pie."

"Put it in the bucket and I'll pull it up."

I found him on the pilothouse bench scooping up pie with his hand and shoveling it into his mouth.

"'Bout time I got some decent cookin'," he said.

For being a pint-sized man, he sure had a loud bark. I noticed that he wasn't wearing his rumpled sea-captain hat and I giggled when I saw one side of his thick white hair sticking up like a porcupine. Must've been napping, I figured.

"I'll heat up the chicken and dumplings for you. But first, I need to tell you about McGuire, the clean-cut prospector."

"What's that?" He set down the pie and gave me his full attention. After I told him what happened, he nodded then puckered his lips. "Need to nip it now."

"Not sure what you mean."

"Find him and ask him square-on why he followed ye. Before he sails with us."

"Won't he wonder why I hid?"

"Don't matter. Kids get scared. Simple as that. Dish up supper, then we'll head in."

IN TOWN, WE FOUND McGuire in a raucous, earsplitting saloon. Cigar smoke choked the room like a smoldering fire. He was sitting at a back table with a dance-hall girl and had a drink in one hand. He noticed us right off as we approached.

The captain planted himself in front of the man.

"Why'd you chase me granddaughter into the stable?" he said in an angry voice.

McGuire squirmed in his chair. "Didn't chase her. Just wanted to talk."

The dance hall girl rose and sauntered away.

"Scared her half to death," the captain said. "What'd ye want that couldn't wait until we sailed?"

He leaned forward, his eyes locked onto the captain. "Something doesn't smell right. Figured the kid would spill it, if pressed."

"Is that so?"

"Don't want any trouble from you, old man. Sit down. I'll buy you a drink."

Please, captain, I prayed under my breath, don't let your thirst for whiskey get the better of you.

"No," the captain snapped, "And stay away from me granddaughter."

"Or what?"

"Ye won't be gettin' a ride to Juneau, that's what. Leavin' at five a.m. tomorrow, sharp."

A man at the next table interrupted. "Did I hear you say you're going to Juneau?"

"Ye did," the captain said.

"Have room for five? Three of them kids."

"Ye don't look like a family man," the captain remarked. He had the normal prospector tattered clothes and a bushy beard.

"Not me. My cousin. After twenty days on the trail, he gave up the dream. Hopes to find work in Juneau, to get his family home. They're good honest people."

McGuire piped up. "His fare is twenty a piece. Isn't that right, old man?"

The captain glared at him. "Ye don't barter me deals." He motioned to the man. "Follow me outside."

"Not fair if you charge me more than him," McGuire hollered as we walked away.

The captain turned around. "This man didn't shoot me boat. And if ye don't watch ye mouth, I'll double ye fare."

On one hand, the captain made me proud. On the other, I didn't think it smart for him to challenge someone so fit. Especially in these parts.

"I don't think we should give McGuire a ride," I said. "You got him riled something fierce."

"It's the whisky talkin'. Hope he keeps drinkin', so he has a queasy stomach when we sail. Maybe we'll feed him greasy food too."

The man inquiring about a ride for his cousin laughed. "Wouldn't want you mad at me," he said. "So, can we strike a deal for my cousin?"

"Ten dollars fer the lot. Plus they bring a bag of potatoes and slab of bacon to share," the captain said.

"Thank you. Awful generous of you."

"One catch," the captain said. "Need his wife to cook. Have 'em at the wharf by three a.m."

"Deal." He reached into his pocket, pulled out ten dollars in coin, and paid the captain.

"Can't say a word to anyone on what we charged. Only to ye cousin. If that prospector asks, I charged twenty a piece fer the parents and ten dollars a kid."

QUARTER TO THREE under a lightened sky, I rowed to the wharf. Shivering in the cold, I wrapped a blanket around me and waited. I waved when I saw the family walking toward me. Each one carried a sack, even the smallest girl. Six-years-old at the most.

"Hello," I said, climbing out of the dinghy. "I'm here to take you to the *Irene*."

"Doyle," the man said.

"Irish?" I could tell by his accent.

"Aye. Me, the Missus, and the clan crossed the Atlantic ten years ago. Except for Katie, there." He pointed at the youngest girl. "She's American-born."

He introduced each one: Mrs. Doyle, Hugh, Mary, and Katie. The children, stout like their parents, had reddish hair and faded freckles.

"I'm Aggie."

"You'll be rowing all of us on your own?" Mr. Doyle asked. "How old are you?"

"Twelve."

"Two years younger than our Mary. Don't see how you can do it."

"I have extra oars," I said as I loaded their supplies. My plan was for one of you to help. I'll take three of you now."

"The kids never lived near water," Mr. Doyle said. "Young Hugh can try. Good for him to learn. He's almost sixteen, but I'll make the first trip with the Missus and Katie. As a youth, I was good with the oars and you've got quite a load with our supplies."

Soon as we got loaded and underway, I was thankful for Mr. Doyle's rowing. He was a bit rusty, but his extra power helped.

"What's the bucket for?" Mrs. Doyle asked as we approached the *Irene*.

"Supplies or any incidentals you don't want to carry up with you on the ladder. We have a pulley hooked to a steam winch. It does all the work."

"My straw doll?" Katie asked.

"Yes, throw it in."

Once we had all the supplies aboard, I decided to send Katie up first and followed directly behind her. "That was easy," she yelled down to her parents.

Next was Mrs. Doyle. Mr. Doyle agreed to follow her up, so there was no need for me to make another trip on the ladder. Sadly, it wasn't easy for Mrs. Doyle to make the climb. It seemed every step required a rest. I was thankful that it was Mr. Doyle pushing on her ample bottom and not me. Finally aboard, she flopped down on the deck and whimpered. Her husband knelt beside her and patted her hand. Captain Murphy looked at me with a what's-this-all-about look? I shrugged and headed down the ladder.

Returning with Hugh and Mary, I spotted Mr. Doyle talking to the captain. It appeared to be a long-winded story. Mrs. Doyle and Katie leaned against the pilothouse and seemed weary and bored.

I walked over to them. "Would you like to go below to the galley?" I asked Mrs. Doyle.

"Below?" she said. "Another ladder?"

"No, we have stairs. It's easy."

When she saw the galley cookstove, she rushed over to it and stroked it like a pet.

"Oh, my," she said. "Nicest I've ever seen."

To me, it looked like a plain old stove. I wondered what she gave up coming to a new country. Then gave up again for Alaska.

"I hope it was explained you'd be cooking?"

Her eyes grew wide and her grumpy frown changed to a smile. "Yes," she said, excited. "Brought potatoes and bacon." She turned to her son. "Hugh, bring down our sacks."

"If you'd like, we have plenty of salmon in jars and canned beans and cherries." I pulled back the cupboard curtains.

"Oh," she said, covering her mouth with her hand.

"Mama," Mary said. "There's a bathtub."

"We fill it with hot water from the boiler. Just have to turn the spigot."

"Such comforts on a boat?" Mrs. Doyle said.

"We don't have these features in our wilderness cabin, but Daddy made sure of it on the boat. My mother called the *Irene* her luxury hotel. Later I'll show you our privy. It's in the pilothouse."

"What?" Mrs. Doyle said.

"Similar to an outhouse, but when the rope is pulled, the rainwater cistern on the roof fills the bowl inside and flushes out to sea."

They all followed me up to the deck for a demonstration, then took turns using the toilet. Having such fun, I had forgotten about the prospector, until I heard voices from the stern. I turned and saw McGuire with another man who reminded me of matted-down wet dog: scraggly beard, wiry hair, and tattered clothes. But not McGuire. He sported a clean-shaven face, combed hair, and presentable clothes.

"Take ye family below," the captain told Mr. Doyle. Once the family disappeared, he turned to me. "Stay here," he said, and then he hobbled over to the prospectors.

"Twenty each," Captain Murphy said sternly.

"Don't think so," McGuire said. "Paid eighty dollars for a Swedish girl and baby. That should cover our fare."

"I had nothin' to do with that. I don't know what girl ye're talkin' about. Sounds to me like ye got swindled."

He waved a paper in the air. "This note from that young prospector lists your boat."

"Don't care," the captain barked.

McGuire paused. "Seems we're at a standstill. You don't trust me, I don't trust you. Maybe we settle on half?"

"Fine," the captain said, "but no meals. And hand over that note, I don't like me boat listed on it."

"Not until we reach Juneau. Where do we squat?"

"Sit in the hold, fer all I care. Pay up," the captain said, shoving his hand toward the prospector.

When I saw McGuire counting out twenty, ten for him and ten for his friend, all in coin, I rushed over with a bucket. He looked at me. "Smart kid," he said. "No meals? Not even coffee?"

"Baaa," the captain said. "Ye can have one plate, but no seconds. And stay out of the galley. We'll bring the food up."

I followed the captain into the pilothouse. "At least we got some money. Should help to buy more wood for this trip. Too bad we can't find a place to collect it for free like back home."

"Aye, maybe we'll be able to work a deal in Juneau."

I wanted to trust that we could, but what I knew of Alaska, nothing was free or cheap.

"Explain to Mr. Doyle about these passengers and tell him to keep scarce."

CHAPTER 13
LYNN CHANNEL

AFTER FOUR HOURS of sailing, black clouds threatened rain and the stale air stunk like musty socks. *Plop, plop, plop* wetted the deck. Plopping faster, it burst into a downpour.

The prospectors, now drenched, jumped up and raced to the pilothouse.

The captain saw them coming, opened the door, and hollered. "Not sittin' in here. Back to the bow."

"Don't be giving me orders," McGuire said, now at the door with the other man. "We're hungry and soaked. Let us in, or we'll trade places with that family below."

"Ye can sit in the shed," the captain said.

The shed butted the pilothouse and housed the boiler drum that stored our steam.

"Not squatting in a shed," the scruffy prospector said.

"Ye will if ye want coffee and another meal."

"Fine," McGuire said. "Better than being out in the cold and wet."

"I'll show them to it," I told the captain. I led them toward the stern.

The shed had u-shaped storage around the drum and was wider at the back, near the louvered half-door. When I pulled the door open, heat blasted my face. "Got blankets around the corner to make up beds."

The scruffy prospector crouched down and crawled inside. "Awful snug in here for two men. Hot and muggy too." McGuire crawled in next.

"Keep the door cracked for air flow. I'll bring up coffee and food shortly." As I walked away, I giggled under my breath and poked my head through the pilothouse door. "Squeezed tighter than pickles in a jar," I told the captain.

"They're lucky we're being hospitable at all."

"I'm going below to check the engine."

Passing the galley, I stopped at the doorway and scanned the room. Seeing the Doyles as a family reminded me of how it was when Mama was alive. Mary and Katie were sitting on my bed reading one of Viorene's books, same way my sisters would do. Hugh and Mr. Doyle at the galley table playing cards. Daddy and I used to play checkers. Mrs. Doyle standing at the cookstove stirring a pot. Cooking and baking on that stove was one of Mama's favorite things to do too.

Mrs. Doyle smiled when she saw me.

"Smells good," I said.

"Potato soup. Good hearty meal. Should be ready soon."

She had made bacon and eggs earlier, but smelling the soup made my stomach growl.

"I'll need two bowls for the prospectors too."

"Thought you were only feeding them once?" Mr. Doyle said.

"Captain changed his mind. Said full bellies means less trouble."

"I agree with that," Mrs. Doyle said. "I'll prepare a tray and have Hugh take it up. Best you not be around such men."

"Thank you," I said. "I do appreciate that. Plus, I have work in the engine room." I looked at Hugh. "They're in the shed behind the pilothouse. Knock on the louvered door."

GOING ABOUT MY chores, I hadn't noticed that Mrs. Doyle had come into the engine room. She startled me when she spoke.

"What are you doing?"

I jumped back and quickly closed the try-cock, stopping the scalding water flowing out into a bucket.

"Bleeding the boiler. Takes concentration." I didn't add that I could've been scalded.

"Ah," she said as if she understood. "You're not a normal girl, are you?" Before she allowed me to answer, she continued on. "I mean you're suited for Alaska. Not a housewife-type like me."

"You seem to be doing fine."

"No. It's all so foreign. Not liking it at all. And I'm worried for my girls. It's so rough here."

"My mother would've worried too."

"Where are your parents?"

After I told her about Mama's passing and Daddy missing, she stepped forward and hugged me.

"You're a strong girl. Wish I was the same. Let me know when you want your soup."

Soon as I stepped into the pilothouse carrying the tray, the captain took it from me, hobbled over to the front bench, and sat down. I stayed at the wheel.

"How's the engine holdin'?" he said, chewing as more questions popped out. "No odd sounds?"

"Seems fine."

Truth was I couldn't tell if it had worsened. With the beams see-sawing back and forth and the rods pumping up and down, I had gotten dizzy watching it and had to sit on the floor.

"Check it every time ye go below," he said. "How are the Doyles doin'?"

"All right, except for Mrs. Doyle. She's unhappy here."

"Takes time."

"No, she opened up to me. I think she misses the farm. And feels trapped."

"Don't be steppin' into things that ain't ye concern."

"I didn't. Just listened, but it got me thinking."

"Conjurin' up ideas again?"

"I thought up a solid plan."

"Is that so?"

"The Doyles can sail home with us, and then catch a train back to Nebraska."

"Trains require money. Did ye think about that? Besides, they sold their farm to get to Alaska. Got nothin' to go to."

"They must have relatives or friends back there."

"Not sure," he said. "The aunt and uncle who got 'em settled died. And their closest cousin is on his way to the Yukon."

"Must be something we can do."

"Ye heart's in the right place, but we can't help every lost soul. As it is, we'll have a full boat—ye sisters, Billy, and maybe ye dad. And don't forget Jake and the goats."

"But the Doyles have lost so much."

"Aye. But to hear Mr. Doyle, Nebraska farmin' was hard. Some years, weevils or a drought plagued the crops and they barely got by. Truth is Juneau's probably the best place as any fer a fresh start."

ENTERING GASTINEAU CHANNEL, the captain had me check the waterline three times.

"Don't want another run-in with ice."

As we pulled up to the Juneau wharf, the stamp mill pounded in the distance. It didn't sound as loud as our visit before. I followed the captain out to the deck. The prospectors stood at the gunwale and waited for the captain to tie the final knot.

It appeared sitting in the shed had taken a toll on them. They stretched. And the scraggly one groaned as he limped off the boat.

"Thanks for the ride, old man," McGuire said, stepping onto the dock behind his friend.

"Wait," the captain said. "Hand over that note," referring to the one Jake had written.

He ignored the captain and walked off.

"No-gooder. Should've known he wouldn't keep his word."

"At least he's out of Skagway and Inga's reach."

"I suppose," he grumbled.

Mr. Doyle and Hugh climbed out of the hatch and headed toward us. "Appreciate all you've done for us," Mr. Doyle said. "We'll pack up and be on our way."

"What's the plan?" the captain said.

He pointed across the channel to an island. "Heard Treadwell might have work."

"Where ye stayin' tonight?" the captain asked.

"Haven't figured that out yet."

"Ye could sleep on the boat," the captain said.

"Didn't want to impose," Mr. Doyle replied, "but that would be appreciated and relieve the Missus."

"We could even dock in Treadwell tonight and save ye the fare on the ferry. A few more miles ain't goin' to tax this boat. Engine's already warmed."

As we approached Treadwell, it looked like a full-fledged town. If it wasn't for the *bang, bang, bang,* it might've been a nice place to live. Long warehouse-like buildings with tin roofs lined the shore. Smaller ones with black stacks spewed smoke into the air.

More impressive were all the houses and storefronts scattered against the hill.

Mr. and Mrs. Doyle walked into the pilothouse. "When does that banging stop?" she asked.

The captain and I stared at each other, but held our tongues. We knew the answer from Jake: two-hundred-forty 1,020-pound stamps, dropping ninety-eight times a minute and running twenty-four hours a day, seven days a week. Only days it didn't was on the Fourth of July and Christmas.

"My sister cut a dozen fabric strips to wrap her ears," I said. "They're in the basket on the galley table. You're welcome to them."

Her eyes welled up with tears.

Right then I felt so sad for her, I almost cried. I knew how she felt. I missed my home, way of life, and the quiet of our homestead.

"Thank you, Aggie," she whispered.

The next morning, Mr. Doyle and Hugh headed off early. In less than three hours, returned with news.

"Got work and good pay," Mr. Doyle said excitedly. "It's a mill-owned town. Got stores, schools, dormitories, and boardinghouses. Even showed plans for a tennis court. I'll be working in the butcher shop. Done plenty of slaughtering on the farm. Hugh got hired in the mines."

"Ain't that somethin'," Captain Murphy said.

"Even giving us housing," Mr. Doyle said. "They deduct it from our pay. If the Missus works in the dining hall, we get free meals. Suppose to stop by this afternoon to sign papers and see our house. Better tell the family."

He and Hugh hurried out the pilothouse door and disappeared down the hatch.

I turned to the captain. "Hope Mrs. Doyle agrees. She's been crying all morning and had to lie down from a headache."

"People get use to the pounding. I'm sure she will too."

After a bit, Mr. and Mrs. Doyle appeared on the deck, dressed in what I figured their Sunday best—cotton pants and white shirt with suspenders for Mr. Doyle. Mrs. Doyle wore a blue-flowered dress, black cape, and straw hat.

The captain and I came out of the pilothouse to greet them.

"Don't ye look nice, Mrs. Doyle," Captain Murphy remarked.

She smiled, but it looked pasted on.

"Should be back in a few hours," Mr. Doyle said. "Kids are instructed not to bother you."

"No problem if they do," the captain said in cheery tone. "The Missus did a good job raisin' those kids. And you'll do a fine job of it here too."

She forced another smile, but when her lip quivered, I pulled the captain to the pilothouse.

"See you later," I said. Once inside, I closed the door.

"Why'd you rush me away like that? I was liftin' her spirits."

"I know you meant well, but I feared one more word and she'd break into an avalanche of tears."

"Oh, wouldn't have wanted that."

When the Doyles returned, I studied Mrs. Doyle's face. She wasn't crying but looked upset.

"How was it?" Captain Murphy said.

"Better than what we had on the farm, right, Mother?"

She nodded, but then her hand flew over her mouth. She raced toward the hatch, sobbing.

"She misses the quiet of the farm," Mr. Doyle said.

"She'll adapt," the captain said.

"Aye," Mr. Doyle replied in a sober tone. "A wagon's on its way now to take us to our new home."

Loading the wagon took no time. The kids said their goodbyes and climbed into the wagon. Mrs. Doyle hesitated then she stepped toward me and hugged me so tight it hurt my ribs. It appeared she didn't want to let go.

"Come along, Mother." Mr. Doyle grasped her arm and helped her into the wagon. As they pulled away, she didn't look back, but I could tell from her quavering shoulders she had broken into sobs.

Tears trickled down my cheeks. I knew it was good they found work and a place to live, but Mrs. Doyle's broken spirit gnawed at my heart.

Treadwell, Alaska
(View of mine buildings and employee homes)

(Courtesy of Alaska State Library, Historical Collections, Louis H. Pedersen Photo Collection, ca. 1905-1915, ASL-P25-093b)

CHAPTER 14
JUNEAU

IT TOOK LONGER to warm our engine than to reach Juneau. Nearing its wharf, the captain closed the throttle and shifted to reverse. When he throttled back on, to let in steam and put the propeller in opposite rotation, the *Irene* froze—dead in the water.

"Rod must've snapped," the captain said. "Lasso to the dolphin," referring to the pilings roped together at the end of the dock.

"Not much more we can do," the captain said. "Let's head to town fer eats."

I debated if I should remind him of our shrinking funds, but decided a few dollars on food wouldn't make a difference.

At the eatery, I sat across from the captain and viewed several women, clad in fancy hats and matching dresses, sitting at a middle table. I wondered if they worked at the dance hall Sadie and Lillie Mae had quit. Three tables beyond, I spotted McGuire with two scrubby men. I quickly looked away.

"Captain," I whispered. "McGuire's here."

"Don't stare. Maybe he won't notice us."

"Too late. He's coming over."

McGuire lodged himself at the end of our table and smirked at the captain.

"Old man. Appears you fibbed to me."

"How's that?" the captain said, keeping his eyes locked on me instead of looking at McGuire.

"Saw a poster on a pole, offering a five-hundred-dollar reward for a missing Swedish girl with a baby. I was told she was a mail-order bride owned by the saloon owner and he wants her back, real bad."

I wanted to scream—that's a lie. She was never a mail-order bride. I stayed tight-lipped.

"Don't know nothin' about it."

"Awful coincidental, don't you think?"

"Way life is. If ye don't mind, like to eat in peace."

McGuire pulled out a chair, sat, and pointed. "That waitress, Maggie, is a talkative one. When I mentioned a man with goats, she knew all about him. Said he was traveling with a group of girls and an old sea captain. What do you make of that?"

The captain faced him. "I wasn't hidin' the fact Jake was on me boat."

"But you pretended the girl didn't exist."

"Told ye all I know," the captain said.

"Don't believe you."

"No concern to me if ye do or ye don't."

"Should be. I figure you owe me passage back to Skagway."

"Ye got your ride at half price."

"And I'll be getting another one for free. Seems I have unfinished business in Skagway." He touched his pocket. "This note has more value than I thought." He stood and pushed the chair under the table. "See you on the boat, old man." He hollered to the two men at his table. "Boys, we'll be sleeping on their boat tonight. Let's go and pick out our bunks."

"Of all times for our boat to be stranded on the dock," I said. "How are we going to keep them off?"

"Can't," the captain said, anger stewing on his face. "This is a real fix. Not sure how to unwind it."

FOR SEVEN DAYS we waited for the blacksmith to fix our part. After I parceled out the money needed, we had only fifty dollars for wood. The worst part—the prospectors used the *Irene* as their flop house.

By nine a.m., they'd head up town, usually to a saloon. After midnight, they'd climb aboard and sleep in the galley. I was forced to stay in the pilothouse with the captain. We barricaded the door at night.

Neither of the two men traveling with McGuire were the same man as before. These men were older, grubbier, and smellier. The heavy-set one had a grayish beard down to his belly and only a few strands on his balding head. He barely fit in our galley wooden chairs. The medium-sized man reminded me of Blackbeard from the picture books—shifty eyes, needle nose, and pointed beard.

"After they leave," the captain said, "go to the eatery and fetch us breakfast. Ham, eggs, and toast."

"How about I fix something here?"

"Ye're good at lots of things, but cookin' ain't one. And if ye're worried about the money, I already worked out a plan."

"What is it?"

"Never mind. And I don't want no pesterin' about it, either."

I prayed he was telling me the truth about the money, but knowing the captain like I did, he could spin a tale better than most. I knew he'd do such a thing to ease my worry. I grabbed a bucket to carry the food in and headed to town.

Every chair in the eatery was taken, so I stood by the kitchen door. A plump middle-aged waitress approached. "It'll be awhile."

"Don't need a seat, just food. Even brought a bucket to carry it."

"Isn't that smart." She pointed. "If you'll pour coffee for those two tables, I'll take your order to the kitchen now."

I completed her request, and as I waited for my food, she asked me to deliver four meals to a table.

"Thank you," she said. "You came in handy."

She wrapped our ham and eggs in a napkin, placed it in my bucket, and dropped two oatmeal cookies on top of the toast. "Dessert as a thank you."

I reached into my pocket, pulled out money, and added an extra coin. "That's for you."

"No honey, don't need your tip. I make enough off these men. Besides, I recognize you now."

"I'm not a regular."

"No, but you did a good deed for my friend. The Swedish girl and the baby."

I stared at her, but didn't say a word.

"Saw you and the sea captain in here the other day. Maggie's got a big mouth," referring to the other waitress. "She shouldn't have told those prospectors about you helping them."

I bit my lip.

"So she made it to Skagway? She and the baby? Where are they staying?"

The captain told me to *never* offer information to a nosy person. To keep my face neutral too.

"Thank you for the food." I turned around and hurried out the door. Running most the way, I stopped to catch my breath before I climbed aboard. I rushed into the pilothouse. "Captain, captain."

"Settle down. Boat's not on fire, is it?"

"No, but a waitress, not the one as before, thanked me for helping Inga and Catrine. Then she wanted to know all about them, but I didn't answer."

"Awful lot of money at stake. Could be a friend or a foe."

"Foe. She didn't call Inga or Catrine by name. Referred to them as the Swedish girl and baby."

"Ye're gettin' good at readin' people."

If he meant not trusting them, he was right. I used to take people at their word. Now I let my gut be the judge.

"Best thing we can do is get the engine fixed."

That afternoon, I checked with the blacksmith again. He quoted five more days.

On my way back to the *Irene*, I spotted McGuire, the clean-cut prospector, coming out of a bank. I ducked behind a crate and waited for him to go into the saloon—his daily routine since we arrived. Instead, he headed toward the wharf.

As I followed from a distance, I stayed on the planked walkway and darted from store to store, ready to dash in, if needed. When I got to the wharf, I raced to the tackle shop, peeked around its corner, and observed McGuire and his two grubby friends. They were standing in a line with about thirty others.

At the dock, a steamer blasted its whistle and dropped its gangplank. That's when I realized the prospectors were leaving on the ship. But to where? I was so engaged watching, I hadn't heard footsteps behind me until a woman spoke.

"What you doing, honey?"

I jumped, spun around, and found myself face to face with the waitress from this morning. She had a tapestry carpetbag in one hand and a black coat draped over her arm. "You scared me."

"What's caught your interest?"

"Nothing."

"Glad I ran into you again. I'm heading to Skagway and would like to see my friend. Where's the Swedish girl staying?"

"Don't know what you're talking about."

She dropped her bag and grabbed my sleeve. "Enough with the games. Where is she?"

I jerked my arm loose and pushed her. As she stumbled backwards, I turned and ran fast as I could to the *Irene*.

I bolted into the pilothouse and up to the captain. "That waitress from this morning grabbed my sleeve and tried to make me talk. I think she's related to the heavy-set prospector. Looks like him. She's sailing on the steamer to Skagway. McGuire was in line too."

He pulled on his chin. "Not good. What'd the blacksmith say?"

"Five more days."

"Out of our hands now," he said in a defeated tone.

As the steamer left port, its whistle blasted again. We watched from the pilothouse window until it disappeared. Bad as it was having the prospectors aboard, it was far worse seeing them sail off.

CHAPTER 15
JUNEAU

THE NEXT MORNING, we waited by the blacksmith's tall stable door. "Want to be the first customer," the captain said. "He'll be in a better mood. Rested and not beaten down from work."

When the heavy door opened, we stepped back.

"Hello, folks," the blacksmith said, surprised. "What brings you by so early?"

"Hopin' to barter a deal," the captain said.

"Barter?" he said as we followed him in.

"Ye quoted one-hundred dollars to fix our rod and another five days. Like to work out other terms."

"If you want the date moved up, it'll cost extra."

The captain reached into his pocket and set his silver pocket watch on the counter. "Would ye be willin' to take this fer payment? Fer the repair and the move up?"

I gasped. "No, captain."

"Quiet, Aggie."

I looked at the blacksmith. "He earned that from the Civil War. Was injured in battle." I pulled out Daddy's pocket watch from my pocket and clasped my hand around it until I mustered the courage to place it down. "Take this one instead."

The blacksmith scowled. "Now I'm being haggled with two watches?"

The captain looked at me sternly. "Aggie, take ye watch and wait outside."

Whenever he called me Aggie, not Aggie-girl, I knew he was serious. I usually obeyed. And as much as I wanted to snatch my watch and race out the door, I had to stand firm. "No," I said. Mine's just as nice and worth the same. Maybe more."

"Now you've sparked my interest."

"My daddy special ordered it from San Francisco. Paid one-hundred-fifty dollars for it. Got it after a good fishing season. It's the type the train engineers use. Calibrated to keep constant time. In any position—even upside down."

He lifted the watch and inspected it.

"If you open the back, you'll see jeweled gears."

"Hmm," he said, carefully opening it. "By golly. Never seen one so nice."

"Aggie," the captain said. "I know what that watch means to ye. We'll figure out somethin' else."

"Hold on," the blacksmith said. "Maybe we can work a deal. To give up such treasures, you folks must be in desperate need for that part."

"We are," I said.

He looked at the captain. "That war was a sad time for this country, but I respect the men who fought. Especially those injured. Keep your watch." The blacksmith turned to me. "But I'm interested in yours. I'll give you a month to buy it back for one-hundred-twenty dollars, otherwise I take possession."

"Thank you. That's awful generous."

The captain pressed his hands down on my shoulders. "We ain't goin' to be in a better position in a month."

"We might be. And Juneau's on our way home."

"It's good ye have a hopeful spirit. But this time ye might be faced with heartbreak. Ye prepared fer that?"

"Yes. Mama taught me long ago that possessions, no matter how special, should never replace people or their needs."

Much as I believed Mama's words, it hurt to be giving up Daddy's watch, but I couldn't let on to the captain. Because as much as Daddy's watch meant to me, the captain's signified even more—a piece of who he was.

"All right," the captain said sadly. He turned to the blacksmith again. "Can we write up a deal and move up the date?"

"Sure can. Rod will be ready tomorrow."

After we left his shop, we stopped at a sawmill, scheduled a wood delivery, and paid seventy-five dollars for half a cord.

"A brave thing givin' up your watch. How 'bout we visit the Doyles and see how they've settled in?"

AS THE FERRY neared Treadwell, the loudness grew. *Bang, bang, bang...*

"Last run, eight p.m.," the ferryman announced.

"We'll be back long before that," the captain told him.

Business after business strung along the shore. Many displayed large signs. Some had directories outlining services and maps.

The captain pointed. "Butcher shop this way. Sign shows it's in the general store."

The general store, large as a warehouse, had shelves reaching to the ceiling and lining every wall. All fully stocked—canned goods, fabric bolts, clothes, shoes, and dishes, to name a few.

"What a stockpile," the captain said. "Do ye see the butcher shop?"

"Clear back there's a skinned cow hanging off a hook."

We headed toward it and waved when we spotted Mr. Doyle. He hurried to us. "Never thought I'd see the likes of you again."

"Waitin' on an engine part," the captain said. "Thought we'd visit. And with luck, we'll be on our way to Skagway tomorrow."

"Why don't you go to the house and visit the Missus? I'm off in an hour."

"How is Mrs. Doyle doing?" I asked.

"Put's on a good face, but worried about Mary. She's awful sick."

"Maybe we shouldn't go then," the captain said.

"No, please do. Company's exactly what she needs."

"Doyle," a voice yelled out. "Need to get this animal dressed for the meat case."

"Right there." He gave us the address and directions, then disappeared behind the cow.

We followed row after row of identical wooden houses, all with white trim. Luckily, each had a large number on the front.

"This one," I said. We barely knocked when the door opened. It surprised me anyone could hear over the stamp mill hammering. Mrs. Doyle smiled when she saw us, motioned us inside, and closed the heavy door. It shielded some of the noise.

"What a surprise," she said, speaking loud. "Thought you were the doctor."

"Stopped to see your husband," the captain said. "Heard Mary was sick. What's wrong?"

"The pounding. It's affected her. She throws up all the time. Even after drinking water. She's sleeping in the corner now."

We followed her to a brown worn-out sofa and sat down.

"Sorry to hear," the captain said.

"According to the doctor, it's common."

"How are Katie and Hugh?" I asked.

"Not bothered. Katie is at a neighbor's. Hugh's working in the mines. He doesn't live here. No room. He's at the hall for single men."

I squirmed on the lumpy sofa. "Couldn't they give you a bigger house?"

"Only one-room cottages available. When it was suggested Hugh sleep at the dormitory, he jumped at the chance."

"Bet he misses the family and ye cookin'," the captain said.

"Stops by every night, but only visits for half-an-hour or so. He doesn't eat our food. They have a real nice dining hall at his place. Nicer than the one where I work."

"What kind of work?" the captain asked.

"Cook's helper. The night shift. I bring home dinner for the next night. They deduct it from my pay, but it's a fair deal. Hope you like chipped beef and gravy."

"Sure do," the captain said as he surveyed the room. "Real homey how ye fixed it up. Once Mary is better, this will be a good life."

"Yes. Has everything needed—a school, church, and a playground with teeter-totters and hopscotch for the girls."

"Seems like a wonderful place to live," he added.

"I suppose." Her eyes grew misty. "For the most part, everything I've told you is true, except Mary is sicker than I let on. Has nosebleeds every day and wobbles as she walks. We were told that was common too. But it doesn't seem normal to me."

I bit my lip and looked at the captain.

"Bet the doctor will have a remedy. Always do. Don't they, Aggie-girl?"

"My grandmother thrived on tonics. Had all kinds to ease her pains."

After the doctor arrived and completed his examination, Mrs. Doyle brought him over and introduced him. We offered to go outside so they could converse, but she insisted we listen. Another set of ears might help, is how she put it.

"She needs to be taken away from here," the doctor said. "Maybe send her to relatives?"

"Don't have anyone close. Won't she get better?"

"Hard to say. One of the worst cases I've seen. Maybe get her to Juneau, away from the loudness."

"Then what?" Mrs. Doyle said.

"With renewed strength, might be able to fight it off or have to live elsewhere."

Mrs. Doyle broke into tears. "We have no money and nowhere to go."

"Let me think on this. I'll check back in a few days." He turned to the captain and me. "Nice to meet you, folks."

The captain nodded. "Same here."

When Mrs. Doyle escorted the doctor to the door, I whispered to the captain. "We could offer a bed on the boat."

He shook his head. "We're only here another day or so. Don't give false hope."

"We could take her to Skagway and bring her back on our way home. That way she'd have at least two more weeks of quiet rest. I'd take care of her."

"Ye forgettin' we might be facin' trouble there? Too dangerous to add a sick kid."

Mrs. Doyle shuffled toward us. Her lip quivered as tears welled up in her eyes again.

"What are you talking about? Do you have an idea? I've been praying for a miracle. Please tell me if you've thought of anything that might help. Please."

The captain sighed and looked at me firmly.

"Please," Mrs. Doyle pleaded. "My brain has run dry."

The captain scratched his chin as he looked up at Mrs. Doyle, but he didn't say a word. But her pitiful face, so sad and stressed, appeared to be melting him down. He cleared his throat.

"We're only in port one more day, and ye husband would have to agree." Before he finished, Mrs. Doyle wrapped her arms around him.

"Thank you, thank you," she repeated through tears. "Stay on the boat. Is that what you're offering?"

"Aye," he said, squirming loose. "But it all depends on what ye husband says. And it might not work."

"But it might. It might," she said excitedly.

When Mr. Doyle stepped through the door, Mrs. Doyle pounced on him like a cat to a mouse. Her arms flailed in the air as she talked.

"Yes, dear," he repeated. "I understand."

"I'll get the food warmed while you discuss the details." She rushed to the cookstove.

"Do you need help?" I asked.

"No. You stay put."

Mr. Doyle sat in a wooden chair across from us. "A lot to take in."

"It unraveled so fast," the captain admitted. "We should've talked to you first."

"No, no. Appreciate your offer. Just need to think it through."

"Nothing to think about," Mrs. Doyle blurted. "I'll pack a bag for Mary and me tonight."

She looked at me. "You're going back to Skagway for your sisters, right?"

I hesitated and glanced at the captain.

"But we might be facin' trouble there," the captain said. "That prospector headed back on a steamer."

"I'll take that chance," she said. "Anything to help Mary."

Mr. Doyle's mouth popped open. "Now wait a minute, Mother. You're jumping the horse, here."

"We have no choice," Mrs. Doyle said. "We have to pull together as a family. And a few weeks on the boat could make a difference. I'll ask Mrs. Watkins to watch after Katie. I helped her when her son was sick."

Treadwell Stamp Mill
(300 Mill, Douglas Island c 1899)

(Courtesy of Alaska State Library, Historical Collections,
Winter and Pond Photo Collection, ca. 1893-1943,
ASL-P87-0376)

After ore arrived from the mine tunnels to the stamp mill, each 1,020 lb stamp, dropping 8-1/2 inches, 98 times per minute, crushed six tons of ore daily. The hammers ran twenty-four hours a day, 7 days a week. The pounding was so loud that people in downtown Douglas Café had to shout to be heard. When the mills shut down for Christmas and the Fourth of July, people reported they could not sleep because it was so quiet. [1]

---

[1] *Juneau-Douglas Mining District, Treadwell Mine Historic Trail,* Published by Taku Conservation Society 2007.

CHAPTER 16
SKAGWAY

WITH THE NEW piston rod installed and Mary and Mrs. Doyle aboard, we set sail to Skagway. Mary was already showing improvement.

I stood at the wheel and glanced at the hook that once held Daddy's pocket watch whenever we sailed. The captain's dangled from it now. I appreciated his gesture of putting it there, but it saddened me whenever I checked the time.

"Another half-hour behind us," I said. It had been ten hours since we had set off. "Going to the engine room."

The captain hobbled over to the wheel. He was antsy about the new rod and insisted I inspect it every half-hour or so. This would be the twentieth time.

I walked into the engine room, headed to the bucket, and reached down for the work gloves. On the side of the boiler were three try-cock valves, water spigots positioned one above the other and four inches apart. To keep from being scalded, they had to be checked in a special order—bottom, middle, top. I scooted the bucket under the spigot, twisted the bottom valve, and as steam hissed and water flowed out, Daddy popped into my head.

"Perfect," he would've said. "Middle one should look the same."

Daddy, not a talker, limited his words, but if a subject interested him, he'd go on and on. Usually those topics included machinery, boats, or a lesson, like the one he had taught me about draining the valves.

When I finished with the boiler, I inspected the engine. It was a triple-expansion and all the parts were multiplied by three: cylinders, piston rods, crank shafts, to name a few. As I listened close to steam hissing from cylinder to cylinder and the piston rods pumping up and down, it sounded like a fine-tuned sewing machine.

On my way to the companion steps—a special staircase that Daddy had built for Mama to the lower deck—I poked my head into the galley. "Look at you," I said to Mary, who was now sitting up on my bed.

"I'm not dizzy anymore. And no nosebleeds."

"That's wonderful news."

"Aggie, come sit." Mrs. Doyle motioned me to a chair next to her at the table. "The captain mentioned you gave up your father's watch."

"I'm getting over it."

"I had to sell my mother's silver cutlery to pay for our Alaska trip. It had been passed down for generations, and was to go to Mary on her wedding day."

"That must've broken your heart," I said.

When she nodded, her eyes dimmed a bit and it made me wonder if every line around them stood for a sacrifice. First, leaving Ireland. That must've been hard knowing you'd never see your family or homeland again. Then, moving from Nebraska. There she had a house and her belongings. And to lose it all for what? A dream her husband had. Right then, I realized how petty I was for fretting over Daddy's watch.

She reached into her pocket. "I'm offering you the money I earned from ironing." She placed coins into my hand. "It's not much. Only ten dollars. But if others chip in, you might be able to get the watch back."

"Thank you, Mrs. Doyle, but I can't take your money." I handed it back to her. "The watch is a trinket in comparison to what you've lost."

"It's not the age or the size of the item, but the value to your heart," she said.

"It was special to me, but I'm letting it go. My family and friends are what's important."

She smiled and patted my hand. "Speaking of family, you must be getting excited to see your sisters. How soon before we arrive to Skagway?"

"Three hours or so, but the captain's insisting I hold off going to town until morning. He feels it's too dangerous at later hours. And with that clean-cut prospector lurking about town, he's probably got spies watching for us, hoping we lead him to Inga."

"What if I go with you?" said Mrs. Doyle. "Then you wouldn't have to wait. We could pretend to be mother and daughter. And Mary's feeling better, so it won't be a problem for her to stay here on her own."

"I am anxious to see them. I'll go talk to the captain now."

AFTER WE ANCHORED in Skagway, I changed into a blue-gingham dress, black tights, and spit-shined boots. Mrs. Doyle braided my hair and tucked it into a blue, wool-knitted hat.

"Be cautious," the captain said, walking with us to the stern. "With people lookin' fer Inga, they'll be watchin' fer strangers and our boat."

The captain had anchored the *Irene* toward the far end of the wharf, so we weren't visible from town, but if they walked the wharf they could see us way off. A robin's-egg-blue boat was easy to spot.

"But they won't be looking for a mother and daughter," Mrs. Doyle added. "We should be fine."

Once we reached the wharf, Mrs. Doyle tucked her arm around mine and guided me along as if we didn't have a care.

When a group of men approached, we diverted into the general store. After they passed, she grabbed my hand, strode us down the block, then crossed toward the music hall. She stopped again, pretended to button my coat, and scanned the street.

"There's a side door around back," I told her.

She nodded, grasped my sleeve, and pulled me with her to the tight alley between two buildings. Soon as we got to the back, I spotted my sisters feeding two stray cats. I called out and raced to them.

Wilmina looked up first, dropped the food scraps, and hurried to me. "Aggie," she said, tackling me in a hug. Viorene raced up and wrapped her arms around us both.

Mrs. Doyle walked up. "Girls, we need to get inside." She herded us in like sheep.

At the kitchen table, Mrs. Doyle removed her coat, draped it over the back of a chair, and sat down.

Viorene hurried off to get Sadie and Lillie Mae. A moment later, the three returned.

After introductions, Sadie and Lillie Mae pecked my cheek and sat down next to Mrs. Doyle. Viorene plopped into the empty chair by Wilmina who was sitting next to me.

Sadie fixed her eyes on me. "Start from the beginning."

I talked and talked and talked. Mrs. Doyle added a few words too. Finally we finished.

"Is the prospector handsome?" Sadie asked. "And clean-shaven?"

"Yes, McGuire is better groomed than most."

"Came in yesterday inquiring about the blonde Dutch girls. Said he saw posters and wanted to know if the act was worth the money. Told him he'd have to see for himself. Tomorrow's their debut."

"What about a plump middle-aged woman with deep brown hair?" I said.

Sadie looked at Lillie Mae. "Just hired one as a waitress. She starts tomorrow tonight. Why?"

"She's with them."

Lillie Mae gasped. "We need to fire her."

"No," Sadie said. "Might cause further suspicion. Best if we come up with a plan."

Mrs. Doyle cleared her throat. "If I may?" She shuffled in her chair. "As a young girl, I wrote plays with twisted plots. Acted them out for my family. Fancy myself pretty good."

"If you got any ideas, let's hear 'em," Sadie said.

"Seems to me, the baby's the link. If they find her, they'll know they have the right girl."

"That has been concern."

"Hide the baby on the *Irene*," Mrs. Doyle said. "If anyone asks, my daughter can claim her. She just turned fifteen, but big for her age. It'd be believable."

"But you were on the boat with the prospector," I said. "He'd remember if there was a baby. And he's pretty smart and would find it fishy."

Mrs. Doyle nodded. "Probably so," she said. "Is there a place that my daughter and I could stay in town to watch after the baby?"

"Plenty of room at my flat," Gertie hollered from the cookstove.

Viorene described Gertie as the happy-go-lucky music-hall cook. She never married, but saved all her money from working in traveling vaudeville shows and bought one of the largest houses in Skagway. She reminded me of Mrs. Doyle in stature, but was much older and her hair was white.

"Thank you, Gertie," Sadie said. "I'll pay you extra."

"Nah, I welcome the company. How many?"

"Three," said Mrs. Doyle. "My daughter and I plus the baby, but we might need to bring Inga. Does she have an accent?"

"Yes," answered Sadie.

"She has to be hidden too. Once that waitress is in house, she'll be nosing around and asking questions of your crew. But you can play her to your benefit and lead her astray."

Sadie laughed. "You are good at this," she told Mrs. Doyle. "What else do you propose?"

"Let me think on that. If you get me paper and pencil, I can scratch out some thoughts."

Lillie Mae stood. "While you're doing that, I'll let Inga know what's going on and to stay low."

As Mrs. Doyle wrote, we glanced at one another around the table, but stayed quiet as mice. Finally Mrs. Doyle spoke. "Inga can still do the act, but she has to be gone before the end of the show."

Sadie shook her head. "They've been advertised as headliners. They have to be at the closing curtain."

"Don't you have any other yellowed-haired girls who could replace her?"

"No," said Sadie. "That's why their act is such a strong attraction."

"I see." She paused and tapped her pencil on the table as if it was helping her think. Suddenly, a big grin crossed her face. "Aggie, how are your dancing skills?"

My mouth flew open.

Sadie jumped up. "Brilliant idea," she said, and then she pulled off my hat. "Perfect color."

"No," I said. "I have no talent." I looked at my sisters. "Tell them."

"She is awful clumsy," Wilmina said. "Trips on rabbit holes all the time."

"After a little practice, she'll do fine," Viorene said. She turned to me. "Remember when I fussed? You told me I had to do it. To help Inga. Same applies to you."

"Are you forgetting that the waitress and the prospector both know my face? How are you going to hide that?" I asked.

Sadie smiled. "With a little make-up and a fancy dress. Just don't show your teeth."

CHAPTER 17
SKAGWAY

MRS. DOYLE EXPLAINED the plan to the captain, and it appeared that he found it sound, but when she got to my part in it, he almost fell off his bench laughing. "Aggie?" He chortled. "In a dressed-up play? Now that I'd pay money to see."

"You can't come," I said. "If anyone saw you at the music hall, they'd know something was up. Besides, it's too dangerous now to leave the boat unprotected."

"I know, I know," he said, holding back a chuckle. He winked at Mrs. Doyle. "Try to get some photos if ye can."

THE NEXT MORNING Mary was feeling so spry, she was anxious to get on land and stretch her legs. "It's been so long since I've felt good, Mother."

"And it's a delight to see," her mother replied, beaming as I rowed them to shore.

It was the first time since we'd met that I truly saw Mrs. Doyle happy. Now realizing how resourceful she was at thinking up plans, I wondered if she had figured out one for Mary.

"I'll see you in two days," I told them. They were heading to Gertie's and I was to stay hidden on the *Irene* until the morning of the show.

OPENING NIGHT we implemented Mrs. Doyle's additional tips: hats, parasols, and masks to conceal.

Viorene sat down next to me. "Ready?"

I huffed. "I feel like a bluebird in this feathered dress. Look how Lillie Mae puffed out my curls."

Before bed, I had rolled my hair in rags. Mrs. Doyle had insisted I needed curls. I was surprised that I hadn't flattened them by wearing my hat.

"You look nice," Viorene said.

"I'm so scared I might throw up." I showed her my trembling hands. "I'm not outgoing like you. Remember how nervous I got at school if I had to speak in front of the class?"

"Take a deep breath."

"Where's Wilmina?" I asked.

"She's staying at Gertie's with Mrs. Doyle and Mary. Sadie thought it was best to keep her out of view. They'll sneak over later to watch the show."

"Good idea to keep her hidden. Especially since McGuire found out about us from that waitress. Only takes one clue to get him thinking."

Sadie sauntered toward us wearing a purple satin gown. With her flaming-red hair curled around her face, a ruby-jeweled crown atop her head, and her cheeks and lips painted rosy red, she looked like a Goddess.

"You're beautiful," I said.

She smiled. "Thank you, Aggie. You're lovely too. You both are."

Viorene grinned, but I shook my head. No point in complaining to her, I decided.

I motioned toward the closed curtain. "Noisy out there."

"Not an empty seat," she replied. "Haven't spotted the prospector, but I'm sure he's here. Where's Inga? We need to go through the plan."

"Right here," coming toward us. She was wearing the same blue-feathered dress as me. Viorene's, the identical design, was green.

Sadie huddled us together. "After I sing *Coming 'Round the Mountain*, I'll introduce you as Etta and Elke, the Golden Dutch Girls."

"Then what?" Inga said, now appearing as nervous as I did. "Do we come out singing or do we wait until center stage? What was our first song again?"

"You don't recall?" Viorene spouted. "We've practiced for over a week."

Sadie interrupted. "Show jitters. She'll be fine once the music starts."

Inga nodded, but didn't look convinced. I knew exactly how she felt—fluttering stomach, chattering teeth, and knocking knees.

"*Two Little Birds Are We*," Viorene said, "That's our first song. We wear feathered masks, stroll out holding hands, and sing."

"Yaaa," Inga said in her Swedish accent, sounding thicker than before.

Viorene continued. "*Sweet Violets* is next. When the banjo starts, off come the masks, but then we're wide open for all to see."

"Hmm," said Sadie. "Don't like that. Thought props were being made? Anyone with binoculars can study your face."

"At least it's a happy-go-lucky number," Viorene said. "We dance and flail our arms all through it."

Sadie frowned. "Just don't stand in place and look out at the crowd."

"A lot to remember," Inga said, wringing her hands.

"You'll be fine, but as soon as you're done, get up to my room and hide." Inga nodded. "Better get to our stations," said Sadie. "Good luck, girls."

Inga and Viorene waited offstage. I squatted down behind a nearby crate with a side view of the show. As the red-velvet curtain opened, Sadie strutted out waving.

"Hello, all." She stopped center stage. "I'm Raging Red Sadie. Welcome." Then she nodded to the piano man and belted out *Oh, Susanna* followed by *Coming 'Round the Mountain.* The crowd stomped their feet, clapped along, and hooted and hollered. Soon as she announced Etta and Elke, the Golden Dutch Girls, the audience hushed.

Viorene clasped onto Inga's hand and guided her to Sadie who then walked off stage. I gnawed with stage fright.

"*Lit-tle bird, Lit-tle bird, sing with me, sing with meee...,*" Viorene sang, holding the last note until Inga chimed in, repeating the same verse. With their feathered dresses and masks, they looked like little birds and brought laughter clear to the last row.

As good as Viorene was, Inga's voice echoed with such sweetness and perfection that she silenced the room. And amazingly, her Swedish accent disappeared. When the girls finished, the people clapped and clapped and clapped.

"Encore, encore," several called out, tossing gold dust onto the stage.

The banjo accompanied by piano started the next song, *In the Good Old Summertime.* Arthur and Charlie, brothers, strode out and joined the girls. Tall with light-brown hair, the boys wore straw hats, white pants, and red and white striped shirts. Arthur latched onto Viorene's arm. Charlie, Inga's. All four strolled across the stage and sang until the orchestra increased the beat then the couples waltzed.

I stood and edged closer to the curtain.

Arthur whirled Viorene around and around. Charlie did the same to Inga and danced her offstage where she traded places with me. As he glided me out, I shook so bad I tripped more than once, but he pranced and bounced up and down as if we were a comic routine. We got good laughs. Once the song finished and the curtain closed and reopened, we held hands and bowed.

Prospectors threw more gold dust at our feet until the floor sparkled like jewels. Soon as we stepped back, the curtain snapped shut, and stagehands with brooms swept up and poured the dust into buckets.

"That was awful. I was certain I might faint."

Charlie shrugged. "A bit clumsy, but we carried it off."

The rest of the show wasn't much easier for me. When not waltzing across the stage, I kept in time to the others as they swayed, swung their arms, and twirled. The show ended with Lillie Mae's operatic song. After the curtain closed again, I lifted up the bottom of my dress and rubbed the sweat off my hands onto my bloomers.

"Stop that," Viorene scolded, tugging my arm until the dress dropped.

The curtain reopened. Viorene and I stayed back, but the audience called out for a special bow. Sadie and Lillie Mae accompanied us to the front. Once the curtain closed again, Viorene and I raced backstage. As we rounded the corner, I spotted the clean-cut prospector talking to a well-dressed man who was smoking a cigar.

"Oh, no," I whispered. "That's McGuire." I pulled Viorene back to the crate. We squatted down behind it and peeked through a crevice.

"He's talking to Mr. Bingham, the owner," Viorene said.

"I demand to see the blonde girls. Got this paper," flashing it in Mr. Bingham's face. "One of them belongs to me."

Sadie saw us hiding and looked at me puzzled.

I put my finger to my lips, then mouthed *prospector* and pointed.

She nodded and approached the men.

"What's going on?"

Mr. Bingham looked at her. "This man's making claim to one of the Golden Dutch Girls."

"Hogwash." Sadie snatched the note from the prospector.

McGuire glared at her and reached for the paper, but she handed it to Mr. Bingham instead.

"Arranged marriages are still carried out," he said.

"Maybe in old countries, but not here," Sadie said. "Besides, our blonde girls are too young to be wed."

"Not the one I'm looking for. She's close to eighteen and has a baby."

Sadie shook her head. "No one here by that description."

"Don't believe you. Give me back that note."

"Now, now," Mr. Bingham said, signaling for Sam and Willie, standing by the door. "Sure we can work a deal."

"No," McGuire said, grabbing for the paper again.

Sam and Willie came up behind him and seized his arms. Mr. Bingham touched the note with his cigar. When it burst into flames, he dropped it to the floor and watched as it turned to ash. He reached into his pocket, took out a wad, counted out one-hundred dollars, and stuffed it into McGuire's coat pocket.

"That should do," he said. "Stay away from my girls." He turned to Sam and Willie. "Get him out of here." As Mr. Bingham walked away, Sam and Willie pulled McGuire to the side entrance, pushed him out, and closed the door behind him.

Sadie hurried to us. "That was close."

Mr. Bingham smiled at us as we stood. "You have the makings to be headliners." He leaned toward me. "You the same girl in rehearsal?"

"No," Sadie said. "You were nowhere to be found, so we had to conjure up a plan."

"Had business dealings out of town, got back right before the show. Best you fill me in."

After Sadie explained the five-hundred-dollar reward, Mr. Bingham turned to me. "Stand-in, eh?"

I cleared my throat. "Yes, sir."

"You fooled me."

"Sir," I said. "I know that prospector. He's determined. And with that waitress lurking around here, you haven't seen the last of him."

He looked at Sadie. "What's this?"

"The woman you hired. We've got someone watching her at all times."

"That won't do. Get rid of her."

"Might cause further suspicion."

"All right," he said. "We'll talk later."

BY THE THIRD night, we had ironed out the show, but with every performance, my knees knocked, my heart fluttered, and my dry mouth craved water. Only good thing about it was all the performers got a cut of the gold dust thrown on stage. Maybe I'll get enough to buy back Daddy's watch, I hoped.

Tonight, as I scrunched down behind the crate, I heard footsteps. They passed me and stopped at the edge of the stage. When I realized it was the waitress, I scooted to the back of the crate, out of her view.

Rapid footsteps approached. "You can't be here," Lillie Mae said.

"Wanted a closer look," the woman said.

Right then, the music changed to my queue to trade places with Inga. I peeked around and watched. As Charlie whirled Inga toward the curtain, I saw him looking for me. Lillie Mae stepped in and strolled with them both back out to the stage.

Sadie stomped over to the waitress. "What are you doing here?"

The woman didn't offer a peep. Instead, she spun around and high-tailed it out the side door.

"Sadie," I whispered. "Is it safe?"

"Who's there?" she said, coming around the crate. "Aggie?" She reached for my hands and helped me stand. After I explained what happened, she frowned. "Knew this trick couldn't last. Especially with all the money at stake. Hide in my room. Let Inga finish the show."

Later that night, we met in Sadie's room. Inga, Viorene, and I sat on the floor. Sadie and Lillie Mae on the bed.

"I spoke with Mr. Bingham." Sadie looked at Inga. "You girls have become so popular, especially you, Inga. But it's not safe for you to stay. How do you feel about San Francisco?"

"San Francisco?" she said. "I'm a farm girl. I wouldn't fit in."

"Mr. Bingham owns an opera hall there. The steamer leaves tomorrow and there's a state room on hold, next to his."

"You can't pass this up," Lillie Mae said.

Inga whimpered. "I don't want to go. You're my friends. I have no one else."

Lillie Mae cleared her throat. "There was mention of me coming later."

"Sadie too?" Inga said in a hopeful voice.

"No," Sadie replied. "In these parts, I'm a Queen, but it wouldn't be the case in a big city."

I wanted to defend her, but deep down I knew she was right. Lillie Mae and Inga sang like angels. Sadie's voice was homespun and suited for clap-along songs.

"How do I get Catrine to the boat?"

"Sam and Mrs. Doyle will bring her to the ship tonight," Sadie said.

"All right, but only if Lillie Mae comes with me."

Sadie smiled, but when her lip quivered, I knew her insides had a different view. I spoke up.

"Inga, that's not fair of you to ask. Sadie needs Lillie Mae. You'll have to go on your own."

"No," Sadie said, with sadness trailing in her voice. "It's too good of an opportunity." She turned to Lillie Mae. "Six months from now, Mr. Bingham might not own the opera house. You have to go."

Lillie Mae nodded. "I'll miss you."

"Not as much as I'll miss you."

HOLLOW, HEARTSICK, LONELY—I knew exactly how Sadie felt. I experienced the same when Mama died. Sadie and Lillie Mae had been friends since girls. As we watched the ship pull out of port, I listened to Sadie's story.

"She's like a sister," Sadie said, referring to Lillie Mae. "Her drunken father and weak mother weren't much different than mine. We took a chance and never looked back."

"It's good you had one another," I said.

She smiled at me. "Like you are for your sisters." She pressed her hand into mine. "Come on," pulling me along. "Let's see if the new posters are up."

Billboards advertising *The Golden Dutch Girls* had been replaced with:

RED, RED, RED
Raging Red Sadie and her Red-head Clan
At the Skagway Music Hall, seven p.m.

"Won't people notice that the Golden Dutch Girls and Lillie Mae are gone?"

"A few might, for a week or so, but they move on and new prospectors arrive."

That night, Zelda, one of the background dancers, wore a floppy hat to cover her brown hair and sang Inga's part with Viorene. Lillie Mae's act got replaced by Sally and Sara, both acrobatic performers, but no operatic songs, instead boisterous ones, like— *Ta-ra-ra Boom-de-ay,* accompanied with girls lifting their skirts and kicking their legs. The prospectors clapped and clapped and hooted and hollered so long and loud, I covered my ears with my hands.

"They sure liked that act," I said to Sadie. "Never seen anything like it."

It's called the French Can-Can. Very popular."

"Why haven't you used it before?"

"We wanted to be more cultured than a dance hall, but with Lillie Mae and Inga gone, our talent has thinned. We're adding six more girls to the dance line. In fact, this Friday will be your last performance."

"Not sorry to hear that, but not sure about my sister. She liked performing."

"It gets in your blood," Sadie said. "Even for someone as proper as Miss Viorene."

CHAPTER 18
SKAGWAY

FRIDAY MORNING, Mrs. Doyle walked into the kitchen with Gertie. "We'll be heading back to the boat after tonight's show," I told them.

"Aye," Mrs. Doyle said, sitting down next to me at the table. Gertie headed to the cookstove.

"This has been a fun visit," Mrs. Doyle said. "Never did I think when Mary and I boarded your boat we'd be helping with a music show and caring for a baby. A pure delight. Best of all, my girl is well again."

"We'll be in port for another few days or so. The captain is hoping for Billy's return. Actually, he should have been back by now."

"So you'll be heading home?"

"That's the plan. The captain thinks it's best to get home before the cold weather hits. Are you ready to go back to Treadwell?"

"No, but it's my fate, but not Mary's."

"What do you mean?"

"She'll be staying with Gertie and sewing costumes for the music hall."

"What will Mr. Doyle think of that?"

"Doesn't matter. She shouldn't be forced to a life of sickness. Besides she'll be of marrying age before long and on her own. I'm just letting her fly early."

I grasped her hand. "This must be hard for you."

"No," she said. "It's the happiest I've been for a long while. And Gertie's wonderful. She's the one who suggested that Mary stay. She's still close enough to visit and the best of it, she won't be sick."

WE'D BEEN FOUR days on the boat since we last performed at the music hall, but we feared the clean-cut prospector, McGuire, might figure things out and think Inga was aboard, so we kept a regimented routine: watched with binoculars, concocted alarms—a bell in the galley and tied tin cans across the stairs. The captain extended our time in port for another week, partly to give Mrs. Doyle more time with Mary but also for the hopeful return of Billy.

This morning I stood at the wheel in the pilothouse next to the captain. My sisters were below in the galley and Mrs. Doyle was sitting on the front bench in the pilothouse conversing with the captain and me. She had already said her goodbyes to Mary and knowing that the captain was anxious to get underway, she didn't want to be the hold up.

Mrs. Doyle pointed out the window "There's a raft coming toward your boat."

I grabbed the binoculars. "Captain, it's Billy."

I rushed to the hatch and yelled for my sisters. We all crowded along the taffrail. As Billy climbed the ladder, I broke into a thousand jittering nerves. *Did he find Daddy? Did he bring him back?*

"Good to see you, boy," the captain said, slapping Billy's arm as he stepped onto the deck.

"Glad to be back. Jake's settling up with the stable owner. Be here shortly."

Before we had a chance to say *welcome home*, Wilmina interrupted. "Is that Hillard in the cage?"

"Sure is," Billy said.

After I introduced Billy to Mrs. Doyle, Viorene headed to the galley to fix him a snack. The others waited for the cage to be lifted aboard.

"Help me with the pulley," I told Billy. He followed me to the mast. "Any news on my dad?"

"Yes. Good and bad."

My stomach tightened. "Bad?"

"Depends on how you view it. Got him to come back with me, but he denied it was him in the photo. Got agitated as I pushed, so I stopped."

"How'd you get him to come?"

"Promised a free ride to Juneau, so he can catch a steamer to Cook Inlet. He heard it's a good place to search for gold. Jake's to stop at the Red Onion Saloon and bring him to the boat."

"Jake can't go into the saloon. He's wanted by that prospector, McGuire."

Billy gulped. "He's still around?"

"Yes. It's a dangerous mess."

Soon as we got the cage onto the deck, Wilmina rushed to it and started petting Hillard. The captain and Mrs. Doyle wandered over to look.

Billy and I approached. "Captain, Billy and I need to talk to you." I motioned him to the pilothouse.

"I'll check on Viorene," Mrs. Doyle said, excusing herself.

"Actually, more ears the better," I told her. "We're in a fix. And you're good with ideas." I turned to Wilmina. "Stay out here with Hillard, but don't you dare open that cage."

AFTER BILLY EXPLAINED about Daddy and that Jake was to meet him at the saloon, the captain grabbed his cap and headed out the pilothouse door.

"Come along, Aggie-girl. Ye'll be rowin' me to shore. Got to get to the saloon and warn Jake."

"What if we're seen?" I said. "The prospector knows us."

He stopped and stroked his chin. "Aye."

Mrs. Doyle spoke up. "He doesn't know me."

"What's that?" the captain said.

"He never got a good look at me," she said. "Use me as the messenger. Wilmina can come along to point out Jake and her dad. And the prospector has never seen Wilmina, has he?"

"That's correct," I said.

"Good. Then we shouldn't draw attention."

"But what if a fight breaks out?"

"Then we improvise," Mrs. Doyle said. "Get your sister ready."

"Ye're a plucky one," the captain told her.

"Have to be in these parts."

Rowing them to the wharf, I instructed Wilmina. "Remember, Daddy doesn't know you. You can't let on or you might scare him off."

"Not to worry," Mrs. Doyle said. "We'll be hand-in-hand."

"I'd feel better if I could come along."

"Can't take the chance," Mrs. Doyle said. "The prospector's seen you dressed up and in overalls. Going to have to trust me and your sister."

"Do you think I could sneak to the music hall? I'd sure love to see Sadie one last time."

"Sorry Aggie, but it'd be too risky. I'd like to hug Mary one last time too, but not sure my heart would survive it again."

"You're right." After I tied onto a piling, I helped them out of the boat. "I'll be waiting here."

I got back into the dinghy, pulled out the old quilt stuffed under the thwart, and wrapped it around me. The whole time I pondered on how to get to the music hall without being seen. It's so close, I thought, but it might as well be an ocean away. Mrs. Doyle was right about it all, the heartache and the risk. After a bit, I saw a man coming. As he neared, I realized he was Jake. I stood up.

"Jake," I said, waving. "Over here." He raced to me. "I'm guessing Mrs. Doyle found you?"

"Yes," he said. "Let's go."

"No. We have to wait."

"But I'm in danger. The prospector saw me."

I wanted to say that it served him right, and to yell at him for the nightmare he caused—all because of greed. But I held my tongue.

I climbed out of the dinghy onto the wharf. "I thought you were bringing my dad with you?"

"Mrs. Doyle is handling it. Can we get going?"

"No. I can't leave them stranded."

"I really need to get out of here. I'm in a bit of a jam with the stable owner too."

"What'd you do? Cheat him?"

"No, but he thinks I did. Not my fault I couldn't bring back his mule and wagon. Had to leave five of my goats behind too. Sold them for the meat and hide. And Horace got eaten by a wolf."

"That's too bad you lost your animals."

"Trail got too harsh to bring them back. Barely got Hillard through. Our agreement was a forty-sixty split of profits, him forty, but he wanted one-hundred dollars more for the loss of the mule and wagon."

"Sounds fair."

"You don't understand agreements."

"I know right from wrong."

"He doesn't know how I got to Skagway. As long as he doesn't talk to the raft owner and figure out my association with your boat, he won't find me."

When we heard voices, Jake jumped into the dinghy, slumped down to the bottom boards, and covered up with the quilt. I hurried away from the dinghy, but turned around when a voice called out. I didn't have a choice, I had reached the end of the dock.

"Hello, miss," a portly middle-aged man said. He was walking toward me with a thinner man. They had passed the dinghy, but luckily hadn't noticed the lump under the quilt.

"Have you seen a tall blond-haired younger man?"

"No," I stuttered.

He looked at me suspiciously. "Sure you didn't see him? Thought he came this way."

"No, sir."

"Odd for a young girl to be out here by herself."

"I'm waiting for my mother. She went to town for supplies. Said I was too sloppy to accompany her."

He chuckled. "Overalls aren't normal attire for a girl, I suppose. Well if you see that chap, tell him the stable owner's looking for him."

As the men walked away, they looked back several times, but I pretended not to notice. Soon as they stepped onto the road and disappeared behind a building, I raced to the dinghy, leaned down, and patted the quilt. "Jake," I whispered.

He peeked out. "Are they gone?"

"Seem to be, but I wouldn't sit up if I were you. I'll tell you this, I don't appreciate having to lie. My mother taught me better than that."

It truly bothered me. The stable owner seemed like a nice man, but I couldn't chance Jake's cheating causing further trouble for us, either. We needed to get out of Skagway without another hitch.

"Figure you owe me a fib." He grinned at me smugly. "Seems I'll be doing one for you."

"What do you mean?"

"Your father. Heard he won't admit to it and I'm to play along."

I sighed and shook my head, then hurried toward the road. I spotted a log, sat down on it, and stared out at the bay. When I heard footsteps, I stood and gawked. It was Mrs. Doyle with Wilmina and Daddy strolling alongside.

My heart raced—*thump, thump, thump.* Trying to control my trembling, I clasped my hands, then walked toward them.

"Aggie," Mrs. Doyle said. "This is John."

"Hello." My voice quivered.

Daddy nodded, but didn't say a word.

"Has Jake arrived?" Mrs. Doyle asked.

"He's in the dinghy."

She and Daddy continued up the dock, but I pulled Wilmina back. She was grinning so wide, she looked like she'd stuffed an ear of corn in her mouth.

"Isn't it wonderful we found Daddy?"

"Yes, but you have to contain your excitement or he'll know something's up."

"I know."

DADDY AND JAKE rowed. Lock-stepping strokes, they got us to the *Irene* lightning-fast. As I stared at Daddy's face, my heart melted. I wanted to hug him so bad. When he glanced at me, I quickly looked away, fearing that I might spook him. Especially if he noticed our resemblance, people always commented how I had his chin.

After we tied the dinghy onto the stern, Jake climbed the ladder first, then Mrs. Doyle and Wilmina. Daddy scaled up behind me. Soon as he stepped aboard, Captain Murphy and Viorene were at his side.

"Hello," Captain Murphy said in a jolly tone. "Good to have ye along."

"Name's John," Daddy said. He dropped his burlap sack on the deck and scanned the boat. "Where's the boy who arranged this?"

"Billy? He's below. Need to speak to him?"

"No, just curious. Appreciate the ride, but it appears you have a lot of people aboard."

"Eight. Countin' you."

Daddy pulled on his lip. If I was reading him right, like I used to, he was mulling over ideas, which usually resulted in a change of mind.

"Awful crowded. Maybe I should go back and wait for the steamer."

"And give up a free ride? No doin'. Ye'll be with me in the pilothouse. The womenfolk stay below and the boys in the shed."

Mrs. Doyle touched my sisters' shoulders. "Come along, girls. Bet these men are starved."

Wilmina hesitated. It appeared she wanted to be near Daddy. I couldn't blame her. I wanted the same, but I couldn't take the chance of her slipping up.

"Go with Mrs. Doyle," I told her.

"Why can't I stay up here with you?"

Viorene grabbed her hand. "Because we need your help fixing supper."

"Anything good to eat now?" Jake said, following them down the stairs to the galley.

The captain nudged Daddy toward the pilot-house. "Put ye bag under the front bench and take a seat. We'll be castin' off shortly."

"Sure there's room for me on this boat?"

"Plenty."

Soon as Daddy walked into the pilothouse, the captain shuffled over to me. "Bit fidgety, ain't he? Best we get movin'."

"Yes," I said. "For Jake's benefit too."

"Aye. That prospector's still loomin'."

"Not just him. Jake and the stable owner."

The captain rolled his eyes. "You can fill me in later." But it turned out, I couldn't.

Voices yelled from the stern. "Lower the ladder."

"Blimey. What now?"

I raced to the taffrail, looked down, and gasped when I saw the stable owner with two men—the raft owner and the prospector, McGuire.

The captain hobbled up to my side. Daddy must've seen us through the pilothouse window, because next thing I knew he was standing with us.

"Been cheated by that young blond chap on this boat," the stable owner said. "He owes me one-hundred dollars and he better pay up. This prospector has a beef with him too."

The captain looked at me.

"That's what I tried to tell you. It's over a wagon and a mule."

"Get Jake up here now." The captain leaned over the taffrail and spoke to the stable owner. "Didn't know any of this. He's on his way."

"Let us aboard and we'll settle it for you," the stable owner said.

"Would, if it was just ye, but that man there," pointing to McGuire, "he ain't welcome."

When I got to the galley, Jake was playing poker with Billy. Mrs. Doyle and my sisters stood at the end of the table cutting up potatoes and carrots for a stew.

"Jake, you're needed up top. It's an emergency."

"What is it?"

"Not sure. I was told to get you right away."

He grumbled, threw down his cards, and headed toward the stairs.

"Should I go too?" Billy said.

"No," I whispered. I waited for Jake to get out of earshot, then I spoke to the group. "The stable owner and the prospector are in a raft at our stern, demanding to come aboard. Stay down here and keep watch," I told them. "I'm going back up top. Listen for the bell if I ring it."

Mrs. Doyle nodded.

As Billy and I stepped onto the deck, we saw Daddy holding Jake in a bear hold. I could tell by Daddy's face that he was annoyed to be involved.

Jake squirmed. "Let go of me." Then he glared at me. "Thanks for letting me know what was going on. Better convince him to release me. Or else."

I knew *or else* meant he'd reveal that we tricked Daddy to come aboard. It appeared that the captain knew what Jake meant too.

"One more threat," the captain told Jake. "Ye're goin' overboard. I'll throw ye me self. Hand over that money."

"No. He got his cut."

The captain reached into Jake's pocket and pulled out a wad of bills. Jake jerked and fidgeted, but Daddy tightened his grip.

"You have no right," Jake spouted.

"I ain't partial to cheaters of any kind," the captain remarked. "Be responsible fer what ye caused." The captain stepped to the taffrail. "Got ye money," he told the stable owner. "Billy will bring it down."

Billy handed the stable owner one-hundred dollars. As he started back up the ladder, McGuire scaled up behind him and raced over to Jake.

Daddy freed Jake, but stayed beside him.

"Got cheated too," McGuire said. "Pay up."

"Mr. Bingham already paid you for Inga." I covered my mouth soon as I said it.

McGuire craned his neck and stared at me.

I gulped.

"Is the Swedish girl aboard? Hand her over." He reached for a gun in a holster belted on his waist. Luckily, Daddy's quick hands grabbed it away.

"There's a five-hundred-dollar reward," Jake told Daddy. "I'll split it with you."

"Girl ain't here," the captain barked. "Now get off me boat."

"Not without my gun or compensation."

The captain scowled. "Jake, pay him another fifty."

Surprisingly, Jake didn't fuss. He pulled out the money and dropped it at his feet. McGuire picked up the scattered bills and stuffed them into his pocket.

"And my gun?"

"After we weigh anchor," the captain said.

"It better be returned," he threatened.

Soon as McGuire climbed down the ladder, we started the anchor winch. When the anchor released from the mud, the captain tossed the empty gun over the taffrail. Within seconds of it landing at the prospector's feet, the raft owner slipped his oar into the water and rowed the raft away. It appeared that he wanted out of this mess too.

"Glad to be done with that scouser," the captain said, referring to McGuire.

I followed the captain into the pilothouse and sat next to Daddy on the front bench.

"Appears Jake has a knack of riling people," Daddy said.

The captain leaned against the wheel. "A schemer. Not a smart trade in these parts."

"But his wits have to be admired," Daddy added.

I was shocked by Daddy's words. The Daddy I knew would've never tolerated such behavior. He would've lectured on the bad of it and what should've been done instead. It bothered me to know he had different views now. I wondered what else had changed.

The captain winked at me, his signal to move ahead with his concocted plan—get Daddy in a conversation so he could hear my voice and look at my face with the hope it'd spark some memories.

I figured it was worth a try, but I didn't count on getting tongue-tied and running out of things to say. Daddy never was a talker. And it appeared having amnesia, if that was what was wrong with him, didn't change that trait. Even the captain chatted to fill in the gaps.

"Say, is that a pod out there?" the captain said.

I peered out the window and smiled. "Looks like humpbacks."

"Probably so," Daddy said disinterested.

"There's one out there puttin' on a show," the captain said. "A lobtailer, slappin' its flukes against the water."

I tried to hand Daddy the binoculars.

He shook his head, leaned back, and closed his eyes.

When I shrugged at the captain, he gave me a sorry-kid-we-tried expression.

"Want me to take the wheel?" I asked.

"My leg could use a rest." He hobbled to the side bench, sat down, and stretched out.

After a bit, Daddy opened his eyes. As he stared at me, it rattled my nerves. "Never thought I'd witness a girl piloting a boat."

I glanced at the captain.

"Learned from her father," said the captain. "He built the *Irene*, but got hurt in a boat accident."

The captain and I watched for a reaction, but Daddy just sat there like a lump.

"Mary Belle," the captain said. "She picked the color fer the hull, robin's-egg-blue. Nice ain't it?"

"Who?"

"Their mother. A Portuguese beauty with olive skin and black flowin' hair. Heartbreakin' when she died."

The puzzled look on Daddy's face made me wonder if mentioning Mama spurred a thought? After all, he had carved her likeness on the prow of the *Claudina*, so we knew some things had come back.

"Sorry to hear." He leaned forward, grabbed his wool coat, and stood. "Need some air."

"Watch ye footin'. Gets slick out there."

"Will do." He brushed behind me to the door. Once outside, buttoned up his coat, pulled out a blue-knitted cap from his pocket, and tugged it down over his blond wavy hair. Then he headed to the bow and stood like a statue, looking out to sea.

I watched him through the window. Tears stung my eyes. "How many times have I seen him do that?"

"Aye," the captain said, standing next to me. "A sea-captain's stance."

"He seemed bothered when you mentioned Mama."

"Might've triggered a memory. Got to keep throwin' reminders and hope more stick."

"Can't we just tell him who we are? And force him to accept the truth?"

"Might come to that, but fer now, it's best to ease him in."

"Wonder if standing at the bow is sparking something?"

"Could. Take him to the engine room next."

"Shhh," I said. "He's coming back."

The wind caught the door as he walked in and slammed it shut. He ambled over to the front bench and sat down. "Cold out there."

"Nothing like boiler heat," I said. "You'll be warm before you know it."

The captain spoke up. "Aggie-girl, bet John might find the engine room interestin'."

"Not the mechanical type," Daddy said.

"It's spectacular," I said. "Something to see."

"Maybe later." He removed his coat and laid it on the bench.

"How about a piece of pie?" the captain said.

"I could go for that," Daddy said.

"Follow Aggie-girl down while I take the wheel."

"Can't she just bring it up?"

"No, she needs to check the try-cocks and the boiler. Could take awhile."

IN THE GALLEY, Wilmina and Viorene sat on my bed, telling stories. Jake and Billy played cards as Mrs. Doyle stood behind them at the cookstove stirring a pan of sizzling onions. The sweet-grilled aroma filled the room and my stomach growled loud as a bear. My cheeks burned from embarrassment.

Jake got up from the table, walked over to us, and extended his hand to Daddy. "Sorry about getting you involved."

"Glad there's no hard feelings," Daddy said. "How 'bout when we get to port, I buy you a drink?"

"Sounds good."

I glanced at Jake, wondering if he was going to apologize to the rest of us for all the havoc he caused. But instead, he headed toward the stairs and climbed up to the deck.

Wilmina sprang out of the chair and seized Daddy's hand. "Come, sit."

"No," he said, sliding her hand off his.

She stared at him then at me. Wetness glistened her eyes. I feared she might break into tears. I spun her around and guided her to the table.

She whispered in my ear. "He didn't want me touching his hand."

"Don't get upset. He's confused. Fix a tray of pie and coffee for three." I walked back to Daddy. "Come see the engine room." He reluctantly followed me.

I put on gloves and headed to the boiler. "My father built and assembled most of these machines."

"Sounds talented." He pointed to the engine. "That's an interesting one."

"Triple-expansion. The heart of this boat. Daddy named a cylinder after each of us girls."

As I threw wood into the firebox, Daddy stood in front of the engine and studied every moving part—the piston rods pumping up and down, the beams see-sawing back and forth, and the cylinders hissing steam.

"The workings of these machines make sense to me," he said in a surprised tone.

"Of course it would. Engines are your passion."

He looked at me quizzically.

"I mean..." As I fumbled what to say, he frowned and shook his head.

"Stop with the games," he said in an irritated tone. "I may resemble him, but I'm *not* your dad."

I wanted to scream *yes, you are.* And your name's *not* John. It's Fred. But I didn't.

"Need air." He stomped away and disappeared up the stairs.

CHAPTER 19
JUNEAU

WITH JUNEAU LESS than an hour away, panic filled inside of me. Daddy had clammed up hours ago. As he sat on the front bench and stared out the window, I stood at the helm next to the captain.

The captain tapped my shoulder. "The photo," he mouthed. After I pulled it out of my pocket and set it in his palm, he hobbled over to the bench and sat next to Daddy.

"John. Need to talk facts."

Daddy faced him.

The captain pointed to the picture and placed it in Daddy's lap. "That's *ye*."

Daddy glanced at it. "No, you're mistaken."

"Known ye over twenty years," the captain said. "Ye're like a son to me. I'm tellin' ye the truth."

I swallowed the nervous lump in my throat, but couldn't do much about the one in my tummy.

"Just look at the girl. She's got ye chin."

He gazed up at me.

"And Viorene has your wavy hair, dimples, and smile," I added.

He turned to the captain. "Stop with the ambush."

"Least ye can do fer the ride and food is the courtesy to listen," the captain said.

"Fine, but I don't recall any of you. Think I'd remember if I had a family."

"Lost ye memory in a boat accident," the captain said matter-of-factly. "Off Cape Flattery. Ye have to admit ye can't remember ye past."

"But some sparks are coming back," I said excitedly. "You carved a likeness of Mama in the *Claudina's* prow. Even added her lopsided smile."

He handed the picture back to the captain. "What is it you expect of me?"

"To come home," I blurted.

The captain held up his hand—his signal for me to stop talking.

"A lot to digest," the captain said. "But think logical about this. Why would we make such claims if it wasn't true?"

"Don't know, but I feel like I'm being pushed into a crate."

"Would ye at least consider our words and spend a few days with the girls? Get to know them. Then decide?"

Daddy scratched his head and puffed out his cheeks. I could see by his face he was calculating thoughts, just like he used to do. He finally spoke.

"If I do that, whatever I decide you'll accept?"

"Seems fair." The captain tilted his face toward me. "Don't ye think, Aggie-girl?"

I wanted to say *NO. What was there to decide? Just come home and adjust.* Instead, I slowly nodded.

"First thing to do," the captain told Daddy, "is to jar that memory. Take hold of the wheel and steer this boat."

"Don't know how."

"Don't give me that. Ye're the best seaman around."

"I'll stay close," I told him.

He cleared his throat, then stood and stepped over to the wheel.

"Just keep her to a steady course," the captain told him.

Standing next to him felt like old times and sure warmed my heart, but he was stiff as an oar and nervous as all get-out. His hands trembled and his forehead beaded with sweat. I tried to relax him by explaining the instruments, hoping that might spur a thought, but all I got from him was: *uh, huh* or silence.

I pointed to the engine levers. "The throttle controls our knots. That's our speed."

"Had enough," Daddy said abruptly. "Why don't you take the wheel for awhile?" He grabbed his wool coat off the bench and headed out the pilothouse door.

The captain took out his kerchief and blew his nose. "Appears to be overwhelmed. Maybe ye should slow down the lessons."

I agreed, but it turned out that it didn't matter because Daddy stayed outside the rest of the trip.

When we reached the Juneau dock, the captain joined Daddy out on the deck. Billy and Jake approached. The captain pointed for them to pick up the lines and help tie down the boat.

I opened the pilothouse door and breathed in the salty air. The freshness cleared my head. The stamp mill echoed in the distance, but didn't annoy me. I wondered if I'd adjusted to the noise or was just pleased about Daddy being aboard.

I grinned at my sisters as they came through the door.

"What's happening?" Viorene said, brushing behind me to the front bench. Wilmina sat next to her.

"We're staying in Juneau a few days so Daddy can get to know us."

"Can't he do that as we sail home?" Viorene said.

I didn't want to upset my sisters by giving them all the facts, so I fibbed. But I crossed my fingers so it wouldn't count as a true lie. "Wants to get the feel of the boat. When you visit with him, be careful with your words and how you act."

"What do you mean?" Viorene said.

"Don't hug him or hold his hand or call him Daddy. It has to be his idea first."

"Didn't you tell him who we were?" Wilmina asked.

"Yes, but he's still uneasy accepting it. But willing to try."

"Girls," Mrs. Doyle said, entering the pilothouse. "I'll be leaving shortly on the ferry. I wanted to thank you for all you've done. I'll never forget you."

"You were a big help to us," I said.

She smiled. "How's it going with your father?"

"He's agreed to stay aboard and get to know us."

She clapped her hands. "Wonderful."

Billy poked his head in. "Mrs. Doyle, I'm ready whenever you are."

"Bags are still below on Aggie's bed."

"I'll get them," he said.

"Best we say our goodbyes," Mrs. Doyle said. She gathered me into a long hug and kissed my cheek. Then went to my sisters and did the same.

When I noticed Daddy was gone, I scanned the deck, then hurried to the captain. "Where is he?"

"Went to town with Jake. Appears they had a truce. Be back in a few hours."

"Are you sure?"

"Stop worryin'." He looked at Mrs. Doyle. "What's the plan?"

Without warning, she wrapped her arms around him. "I'll never be able to thank you enough," she said, tears trailing down her cheeks.

"Now, now," he said, squirming loose. "All the grand cookin' alone saved us. Need help gettin' home?"

"Billy already offered."

"Aggie-girl, why don't ye go with them? Do ye good to get off this boat."

"Shouldn't I be here when Daddy gets back?"

"No. It'd be good fer him to get to know ye sisters. Maybe they'll be able to strike a match in his head."

I agreed to go, but it didn't stop my what-if worries: *what if* he catches the steamer to Nome without coming back to our boat? Or, *what if* he stays in town and hides out. My head was filled with all kinds of *what-ifs*. None of them good.

AS THE FERRY neared Treadwell, the pounding grew—*bang, bang, bang*. I looked at Mrs. Doyle. Her face clouded with fret. Billy and I followed her off the ferry and carried her baskets. The walkway through town winded up the hill, around a corner, and to rows of cottages that all looked alike.

"Here we are," Mrs. Doyle said, pushing the heavy door open. We hurried in behind her and closed out the noise.

"A lot quieter in here," Billy said. His eyes locked on Katie who was sitting at the table.

Mrs. Doyle rushed to her.

"Mother." Katie tried to stand, but her legs buckled and she fell back into the chair.

Mrs. Doyle knelt down next to her. "Katie?"

"No nosebleeds. Just my balance. Started after you left."

Mrs. Doyle gasped. "Sweet child. I would've never left you behind, if I'd known. Where is Mrs. Watkins? I thought she was watching after you. And how are your brother and dad?"

"Mrs. Watkins checks on me every hour and Daddy and Hugh are both fine. The noise hasn't affected them. The doctor said it has to do with my inner ear. Gave me medicine."

"Is it helping?"

"Yes. He says it's common. Not like what Mary had."

Mrs. Doyle bit her lip, stopping the tears ready to cascade down her cheeks. "I'd never let that happen," she said, stroking little Katie's hair. "I'm good at figuring things out." She tilted her head up. Her lip quivered. "Aren't I, Aggie?"

"Yes. You're one of the cleverest people I know."

CHAPTER 20
JUNEAU

IT HAD BEEN TWO days since Mrs. Doyle had left and I thought about her often, but I knew if I brought up any worries, the captain would scold me good. On the positive, Daddy was coming around. He listened to our stories, told some himself, and even let Wilmina snuggle up next to him as Viorene read aloud. Tonight, Wilmina fell asleep on his lap. He carried her to bed and tucked her in.

"See you in the morning," he said.

We listened as he stomped up the stairs.

"It's wonderful having him back," Viorene said. "Even if he doesn't know us, he's learning to love us."

I nodded and hoped she was right, but I had concerns—nightly visits to the saloon, for one. That's where he was heading now. Daddy never gambled, calling it a wasteful use of a man's time. Now he had taken it on as a habit and was letting Jake tag along. When I questioned the captain about it, he said for me to give him time. Said the brain still had un-swelling to do.

"I'm going to the pilothouse," I told Viorene.

"Send Billy down for a lesson," she said.

She had taught Billy the alphabet, how to write his name, and to do simple add and subtract. He sure was devoted to her. To Viorene, he was a project but she also considered him a friend. Always room to improve, she'd say. He never fussed, even when she was teaching him how to fold a napkin or hold a fork.

I walked into the pilothouse. "Viorene's waiting to teach you something new," I told Billy.

"Good." He hopped off the bench and headed out the door.

The captain lowered his peg leg and scooted over for me to sit on the front bench. "How was the visit with ye dad?"

"Fine. Even kissed us goodnight."

"That's a grand sign."

"I suppose."

"Ye don't sound convinced. What's wrong?"

"We're leaving the day after tomorrow and he still hasn't committed."

"Aye, but he appears to be makin' a turn."

"Hope so."

"Did I ever tell ye the time I almost got eaten by a killer whale?"

"No."

"Quite an adventure."

I knew he was trying to divert my attention, to get me off the worry road. I appreciated his effort and played along. Could he spin a tale, this one was especially good.

"That whale's teeth, sharp as any I'd ever seen, took a bite out of my rowboat," he said. "Almost caused me to sink. Never rowed so fast in my life."

The story went on and on and was fun to hear. I had to admit he eased my worry, but I woke more than once that night from a nightmare about giant teeth.

The next morning, Daddy, Jake, and Billy left for town. Said they had goods to buy. When I inquired about it, I was told to never mind.

"Don't want to ruin the surprise, do you?" Daddy smiled wide and patted my head.

It was the first time since the getting-to-know-us-again stage that he appeared relaxed and truly happy. Could this mean he'd settled on coming home with us? Sure is acting that way. I wanted to share my excitement with my sisters, but cautioned myself to not. How many times had I given positive news to have it turn out the opposite? No, I had to be patient. Not a virtue of mine, but I had to do it.

"Wonder what it might be?" I said to the captain. "You have any ideas?"

"No. Wouldn't tell ye if I did. Surprise means surprise."

"All right. I'll try to constrain."

He chuckled. "Look forward to seein' that."

DADDY'S BIG SURPRISE was a crab feast. I contained my disappointment, but the truth was I thought he was bringing back personal gifts—maybe a doll for Wilmina, a book for Viorene, and a sketch pad for me. When I had told him I liked to draw he appeared delighted. He even had me do a sketch of the boat.

He rubbed his hands together. "Let's fire up the boiler and get these kings cooked."

King crabs have the same ten legs as Dungeness—four on each side and two front claws, but are a whole lot bigger.

"Awful nice surprise," the captain said. "Got enough here to last days."

"Fresh off the boat. That's why I needed the boys. Couldn't move this barrel myself."

The captain smacked his lips. "Fill up the hold with sea water. Dump half the live ones there and cook the rest."

Once Daddy, Billy, and Jake got the barrel aboard and teetered it across the deck to the stern, I called for my sisters to come up. After we relayed pails of sea water to fill up the hold, Daddy and Jake tilted the barrel over and poured out half of the spiny crabs. *Splash, splash, splash.*

With gloved hands, Daddy threw four giant crabs into the washtub of scalding water piped from the boiler. Soon as their shells changed to bright orange, we knew they were cooked. Holding the long-handled prongs, Daddy fished out the crabs, piled them onto a platter, and added four more to the cooking tub.

"Better get them while they're hot," he said.

I handed out tin plates and pliers for cracking, then plopped down on the deck and completed a half-circle with Viorene and Wilmina on one side of me, Jake and Billy on the other. Daddy and the captain sat across on up-side-down metal buckets.

"Knew any daughters of mine would find this a treat." It was the first time he referred to us as his daughters. And the first time I called him Daddy to his face. He didn't seem to mind. I had to admit, it spurred my hope. The captain winked at me. I smiled back. This *was* a far better gift after all, I decided.

"Who wants more?" Daddy said.

"I do, I do," Wilmina said.

"I'll have some," Viorene said, politely. She ended her sentence with a thank you as he placed a crab leg on her plate.

The afternoon rushed by. I didn't want it to end. It was the first time since Mama died that we connected as a family and it felt like home.

"Better clean up," Daddy said, gathering our dishes. "Jake and I got a card game tonight. With high stakes."

With that news, my spirits deflated. I had hoped the kinship would last until bedtime. Maybe he'd read us a story. The captain gave me one of his quit-worrying looks. He could read my face better than my sisters could, even when I tried to look neutral.

"Sounds excitin'," the captain said.

"Wanna come?" Daddy asked him.

The captain gambling? Oh, no, I thought. In the past, it always brought him trouble.

"Well... sounds awful temptin'."

I interrupted. "Maybe you shouldn't. You're still recovering from losing your leg."

"Hogwash. Think I will go. What do I need to stake a bet?"

"Five dollars should do," Daddy said.

The captain pulled me aside. "Could ye spot me the money?"

"Uh...sure." How could I not with all he'd been through trying to help us? "Want me to come along?"

"No. Don't need no babysitter."

The captain followed me to the pilothouse where I'd stashed a gunnysack of bills. I counted out the money and placed it in his hand.

"Get that worry off ye face. Just men havin' fun. Nothin' wrong with that."

"Uh, huh." Not believing one breath of my reply.

"Don't wait up." He hobbled out the pilothouse door.

Billy strolled up to me. "Don't worry, Aggie. I'll go and keep watch."

"All right," I said, with hesitation. Now I worried about Billy. He hadn't pickpocketed since coming along, but people could be tempted if situations allowed. I learned that from traveling in these parts.

"Not goin' to steal, if that's your concern."

"Didn't say you would," I replied, but it appeared my easy-to-read face did. And as quick as a lightning strike, the men disappeared off the boat and headed off like partners up to no good. I balled up with worry. I tried to calm myself, but couldn't.

THREE HOURS AFTER they left, I waited in the pilothouse and thumbed through a *Frontier Story Magazine.* One article told about bear hunting. I knew enough about that from accompanying Daddy in the woods. It appeared factual. Another one featured life in an Arizona cowboy town with rattlesnakes, dust, and blazing hot days. But nothing compared to what we were witnessing in Alaska—prospectors, gambling halls, and gold-dust greed.

When I heard footsteps, I stood and saw Billy racing across the deck.

"What's wrong?"

"Captain got into a fix. Betted more than he had. Luckily, your dad won the hand, but the captain blurted out he didn't need no favors, had the money stashed on the boat."

"I knew this wouldn't turn out good."

"I saw three men at the next table had overheard and were eyeing one another. Your dad saw them too, excused himself, came over to me and told me to hightail it here. Wants you to get the boat moved and docked at Treadwell."

"So they're letting us fend for ourselves?"

"No, they're coming, but figured I'd be faster getting the message to you. Said if you're gone, they'd catch the morning ferry and hopefully avoid a fight."

"Need the lines untied," I told Billy. "Take the bow. I'll get the stern. Cut them if you have to."

I yelled down the hatch to my sisters. "Need help." A moment later, Wilmina charged ahead of Viorene and skidded to a stop next to me. "Finish untying while I get the engine started."

I dashed to the pilothouse. No sooner were the lines untied and thrown onto the deck, when I spotted three men coming up the wharf. Luckily, we had banked steam and warm cylinders. As the men neared, I full throttled, pushed the lever forward, and the *Irene* sputtered from the dock. Billy and my sisters piled into the pilothouse. Wilmina stood next to Billy at the window. Viorene sat down on the front bench.

"Give me the binoculars," Billy said to Wilmina. He focused the lenses on the men. "Yep, that's them."

"Hope they don't think to look at Treadwell," I said, spinning the wheel with trembling hands.

Billy continued observing the men. "They haven't moved. Seem to be studying our direction."

"Great," I said in an irritated tone. "Now our only hope is the ferry has made its last run. What about Daddy, Jake, and the captain? See them?"

"Sure do. They're standing above on the street watching us. Now they're turning around. Must figure we're safe, so probably heading back to the saloon. But...those men haven't budged."

Treadwell, Alaska
(Treadwell mine buildings along waterfront,
Douglas Island. Juneau in background)

*(Courtesy of Alaska State Library, Historical Collections,
William Barquist Photo Collection, ca. 1895-1935,
ASL-P164-18)*

CHAPTER 21
TREADWELL

EVEN WITH NO FERRY until morning, Billy and I took turns as lookouts. When the morning ferry arrived, Billy and I stood at the gunwale and observed every passenger who debarked. My sisters stayed below.

"Don't see the men from the saloon," Billy said. He pointed. "But I see your dad, Jake, and the captain stepping off."

After they boarded the *Irene*, I stared at the captain. His face drooped like a hound dog. If I hadn't been so angry, I would've laughed. He held up his hand.

"Don't want no talkin'." He hobbled toward the pilothouse.

The rest of us followed him inside. I sat next to Daddy on the front bench and Jake leaned against the wheel. Billy assisted the captain onto the back floor mattress, then went outside, saying he needed air to wake up.

"Smart thinking to have us move," I told Daddy. "Those men were minutes from jumping aboard."

"Glad you got away."

"We feared they might've caught the last ferry, so we kept all-night watch," I added.

"They'd never come to Treadwell," Jake said. "Too much protection here from the mill guards, but they could get off at Douglas and walk it."

"Stop worryin' her," the captain snapped. "We're safe now."

I stood. "Anyone for coffee?"

"Maybe in an hour," Daddy said. "Need a nap."

"Later fer me too," the captain added.

"How about you, Jake?"

"No. Need to check on my goat, then I'm heading to town for a bite."

"Your goat?" I remarked. "Wilmina said you gave Hillard to her. She's been feeding and combing him and putting down new hay for his bed."

"Told her that back on the mountain. It doesn't apply now."

"Afraid it does," the captain said. "All the turmoil ye caused, ye owe her that goat. If ye don't agree, ye'll be walkin' back to Wrangell. Better make good on the wood you promised us too."

He huffed. "This whole trip was a bust. Be back by noon."

"Make sure you are," the captain said.

AFTER AN HOUR, I brought up coffee and biscuits. "Billy is taking Viorene and Wilmina to see Mrs. Doyle," I told the captain. "My sisters have never been to their house and wanted to visit and say goodbye to Katie too. They'll be back in an hour."

"Fine by me," said the captain.

Daddy sat up. "Smells good. Pour me a cup, please." He rolled up his mattress and tucked it under the bench, then stood and stepped to the wheel. I handed him his coffee. He swallowed down half, asked for more, and grabbed a biscuit off the tray.

"Would appreciate some attention back here," the captain said.

"All right, but not sure you deserve it." I placed the tray on the floor by his mattress and sat down on the nearby bench.

With two swigs of coffee in his belly and a half biscuit, he finally spoke. "I messed up. Ye were right to worry."

"Are you feeling better?"

"Except fer the headache, back to me old self."

Daddy sat down on the bench next to me. "How can people stand living in Treadwell?"

"Not helpin' with me head, that's fer certain," the captain said.

Daddy looked at me. "Aggie, I need a word with the captain. Alone."

"Oh...All right. I'll go below."

As I walked out of the pilothouse, I knotted up with worry. Based on past experiences, nothing ever turned out good when adults talked in private. I debated on what to do. Do I listen in? Or do the proper thing and wait in the galley? Much as I knew I shouldn't, I ducked below the pilothouse side window, crept to the boiler shed, opened the louvered door, and crawled inside. As I slithered around the boiler drum, my heart thumped and thumped. When I got within earshot, near the opening to the pilothouse, I froze and listened.

"Aye," the captain said. "This is a fine boat. The best ye ever built, but that isn't what ye wanted to talk about it, is it?"

"No," Daddy said. "Trying to get up my nerve."

"Spit it out."

"It's like this," Daddy said. "I'm pleased to have such fine daughters, but ...." He sighed then sighed again. "I'm not the same man they remember."

"Believe they understand that," the captain said.

"Aggie and Viorene might, but not Wilmina. She clings to me. It puts me at unease."

"We can tell her to hold back."

"No. They all have expectations I can't meet. I enjoy gambling and I'm still thirsty to find gold."

"What are ye saying, John?"

He cleared his throat. "First, thank you for calling me that. May not be my given name, but it's the only one I know."

"How do ye feel when the girls call ye Daddy?"

"Suffocated, like I'm being gobbled up by the past."

I covered my mouth with my hand to hold back a whimper, but I couldn't stop the tears stinging my eyes. I got sick. Real sick. Not the throw-up kind, but the type that rips out a heart.

"Daddy comes with responsibility. I don't want it. Maybe if more memories return, I'll feel different."

"Aye." I heard sadness lagging in the captain's voice. "What do ye propose?"

"Get papers drawn up giving you guardianship and sign over all my assets to the girls."

"Should be doable," the captain said. "I'm sure this town has the proper authority."

"That was my thinking," Daddy said. "I'd like to get moving on it now. I don't want to masquerade anymore and cause them more pain."

"They will be hurt by this. Might be best fer ye to sit with them and explain."

"I can't. Too much of a coward. I was hoping you'd do it."

At that moment, I wanted to scream out—how dare you sign us away? Instead, his betrayal assaulted me so deep I went numb.

"Let's get Aggie up here," the captain said. "I'll tell her we have business to conduct."

I scooted backwards, opened the door, and slid out onto the deck. I stood and hurried to the taffrail, leaned against it, and looked out at a flock of seagulls, squawking and flapping away. After a bit, I heard the captain's peg leg striking the deck.

"There ye are. Was ringin' the bell in the engine room."

I wiped the tears from my face with the back of my hand, turned around, and faced him.

"Did you and Daddy have a good talk?" I stammered. Then without warning, I unraveled into stuttering sobs, trying to catch my breath in between.

He opened his arms. "Come here."

Soon as I stepped within his reach, he pulled me to his chest and I cried and cried and cried. He rocked me back and forth and didn't talk for the longest time. As my weeping slowed, he whispered in my ear. "Were ye listenin'?"

I nodded.

"Saves me from havin' to break it, I suppose. Come along." He ushered me into the pilothouse and up to Daddy, now standing at the wheel.

"Guess ye won't be spared."

Daddy squinted. "What do you mean?"

"She was listenin'. Heard every bit."

His face went blank—no smile or frown. "I'm sorry, Aggie." He reached for my shoulder, but I jerked it back.

"Don't touch me. You're not my father. My father would *never* abandon us."

He gave the captain a pleading look.

"Aggie," the captain said. "Ye have to be brave."

"Why?" I screamed.

"Because ye're the captain of this boat," he said sternly.

"That doesn't make sense. I'm just a kid."

Daddy brushed past me. "I'll meet you on the wharf," he told the captain. He picked up his burlap sack, opened the pilothouse door, and hurried out.

"With all ye endured on this trip, ye kid days are long gone. Ye think more like an adult than most grownups I know. Should be proud of that fact."

Stock-still, as if I'd been hit in the head, I stared at him and bit my lip. I tried to take in his words, but I was too upset to hear. I slumped down onto the front bench and unleashed a waterfall of tears. I couldn't stop.

The captain sat next to me and stroked my hair. "That's all right, Aggie-girl. Cry it out."

"I don't want to," I spouted. "He doesn't deserve my tears. How dare he throw us away."

"Aggie, look at me." He put his finger under my chin and turned me to him. "That man out there ain't ye dad. And as much as ye want to force him into old shoes, they don't fit no more. Ye know I'm right."

I sucked in my cheeks and gave him a don't-make-me-admit-that look, but he stared me down until I nodded.

"Now ye gotta be strong. Think ye can do that?"

I shrugged.

"Trustin' ye can. Be back in an hour or so."

By the time my sisters and Billy returned, I had cried myself dry. I was thankful for that, but I didn't have the strength to tell them what had happened.

"Where's Daddy?" Wilmina asked.

"He and the captain went up town." I quickly changed the subject. "Did you have a nice visit?"

"Yes," Viorene said. "The Doyles have a cozy place and the pounding doesn't echo as much as it does on this boat, but I wouldn't want to live there."

"Me neither," I said.

"You feeling all right?" Viorene asked. "Your eyes are bloodshot."

"Lack of sleep. I need a walk."

I had gone farther than intended. When I saw the captain coming, I tried to duck behind a bush, but he spotted me first and signaled for me to wait.

"Where's Daddy? I mean John."

"Be along shortly. Needed items from the general store."

"Is he at least going to say goodbye?"

"Not sure. How ye holdin' up?"

"Still numb."

As Daddy approached, it took every bit of courage I had to smile. He grinned at me, then looked at the captain. "Everything in order?"

"Sealed in this envelope." The captain patted his coat pocket. "Good idea on gettin' ye picture taken and havin' it notarized."

"Figured it'd be a good comparison to my sea captain's license. Still can't believe that's me."

Daddy turned, stepped toward me, and pressed his hand on my shoulder. "I do love you. If I didn't, it wouldn't hurt so much to leave."

I wanted to say, "then don't!" Instead, I straightened and looked at him square-on. "I love you too. Will you visit someday?"

"Sure you want me to?"

"Yes."

"Should be easy to find you. Not many places called Humptulips or boats like the *Irene*."

I swallowed the lump from my throat and nodded.

"Probably best I go ahead and catch the ferry without being seen by your sisters."

I wrapped my arms around him. He stood motionless, then dropped his burlap sack and flung his arms around me. He hugged me so tight it squeezed the air from my lungs. As he stepped back, I saw a stray tear falling down his cheek. He didn't try to hide it.

"So long for now," he said. He turned to the captain and shook his hand, then leaned down and kissed my cheek. He picked up his burlap sack and walked away.

My chin quivered.

The captain patted my back. "Ye did good, Aggie-girl. Real good."

Watching Daddy springing up and down with his trademark grasshopper steps, getting farther and farther away, ached at my heart, like it was being ripped in two. I swiped away the tears streaming down my face.

"It used to be so simple when Mama was alive. Why'd Daddy have to change? Then change again?"

"Way life works," the captain said. "At least we found him." The captain reached into his pocket and pulled out a packet wrapped in cloth. "This is from ye dad. He told me to give it to ye whenever I figured the time was right."

"What is it?"

"No idea."

I carefully unfolded the cloth. I gasped. "Daddy's watch. How'd he know?"

"I may have mentioned it the night we went gamblin'. I was tryin' to win enough money to buy it back. He must've got it before we caught the mornin' ferry."

"There's a note." I opened it, took a deep breath, and read it aloud.

Dear Aggie, Viorene, and Wilmina –

Please forgive me for leaving. I do it with a heavy heart. At the strike of noon, think of me daily. I will do the same of you. My hope is these reminders will make my memories stronger and maybe lead me home.

I love you - Dad

The captain pulled me to him. Just then, an albatross flapped its long wings above us. I gazed up and watched.

"That funny bird appears to be our lucky charm," the captain said. "It was one that led us here."

"Yes," I said, thinking back to that day when I wasn't sure which direction to point the boat until I saw an albatross soaring above us.

"This one seems to be tellin' us time to go," the captain added. "Those birds are so clumsy on land, how they stumble over their own feet, but look how magnificent they are in the sky, spannin' their wings and soarin' high above."

I brushed the wetness off my cheek with my coat sleeve. "Daddy used to call the *Irene* an albatross. I thought of myself as one too. Maybe Daddy's one now and he's meant to trip a bit before figuring things out."

"Could be, Aggie-girl, could be. Smart as an old hoot owl, ain't ye?"

"If you say so."

"Ye're the captain of the *Irene* now. Ye earned it on bravery alone."

"Not sure if it was that or pure survival, but I do know that it's time for me to set my own course. Be like an albatross and soar for home."

"Believe so."

"You were right," I told him. "Much as I wanted to keep things the same, life marches on its own path. And you just have to go along with both the good and the bad."

"Hard lesson to swallow," the captain said. "But faced by all of us."

I tucked the watch into my overalls top pocket. As I felt it ticking in rhythm to my heart, I smiled. A comforting thought popped into my head—the next time this watch leaves my side, Daddy will be home, and I'll be placing it in his hands...for keeps.

RESOURCES

The Alaska Sportsman, October 1954, Man the Pumps! by Fred Cline as told to Paul Taylor. (Fred Cline was the author's great-grandfather.) Fred Cline's quote in the magazine on his Alaskan voyage on the *William J. Bryant* to Cook Inlet in 1896:

> *"On every one of those days, I cursed myself for leaving Cook Inlet. To this day I swear I wouldn't have left if I'd had any money, for I was beginning to feel a touch of gold fever."*

Alaska State Library - Historical Collections - digital archives #6487. (Permission granted to use pictures on pg: 12, 38, 53, 54, 65, 66, 77, 78, 101, 102, 145, 164, 221) https://vilda.alaska.edu/digital/search

Angora goats:
https://digitalcollections.lib.washington.edu/digital/collection/alaskawcanada/id/1120/rec/4
(University of Washington Libraries, Special Collections).

As Precious as Gold - Stories from the Gold Rush Trails
https://postalmuseum.si.edu/exhibition/as-precious-as-gold-stories-from-the-gold-rush/the-trails
(Smithsonian, National Postal Museum)

Beatrice Lorne billed as "The Kondike Nightingale" known for her exquisite soprano voice.

Treadwell Mining Complex
http://www.juneau.lib.ak.us/history/documents/Tread
wellMiningComplexHistoricResourcesSurvey-
reduced.pdf.

Berton, Pierre, 1958, *Klondike Fever,* Basic Books, NY
Chapter 4, Pg 165: The average man carried about sixty-five pounds, moved it about five miles, cached it, and returned for another load, continuing this laborious process until the entire ton of supplies was shuttled across the pass.

Provenson, Alice, 2005, *Klondike Gold,* Simon & Schuster, Children's Publishing Division

GLOSSARY

AFT/ASTERN: TOWARD THE STERN; the back.

BAR: USUALLY AN ENTRANCE of a river or harbor that is plagued with mounds of sand formed by the sea.

BATTEN DOWN: PREPARING FOR ROUGH SEAS or weather by closing all portholes, hatches, and other openings on a boat.

BERTH: BED OR BUNK in a boat.

BILGE WATER: A MIXTURE OF SEA WATER, fresh water, oil, and sludge.

BLOCK: A PULLEY on a boat for directing line.

BOILER: AN ENCLOSED VESSEL, USUALLY CAST-IRON. Its main function is to convert water to steam to power the engine.

BOILER DRUM: TANK that stores the steam.

BOILER PEEP HOLE: A SMALL OPENING used to check the fire without opening the firebox door.

BOW: THE FRONT of a boat.

BULKHEAD: A WALL within the hull of a boat.

CAST OFF: TO LEAVE a dock; let loose the lines.

CHART: NAUTICAL MAP.

COCKBILLED: AN ANCHOR SET AT AN ANGLE as it hangs over the bow ready to be dropped.

COURSE: DIRECTION a boat is being steered.

DINGHY: A SMALL ROWBOAT carried or towed by a larger boat.

DOLPHIN: PILINGS TIED TOGETHER.

DOCK: A FLOAT, pier, or wharf.

ENGINE ROOM: ROOM that houses the boiler, engine, steering gears, etc.

FIREBOX: BOILER FURNACE.

FISHERMAN ANCHOR: ALSO KNOWN as Admiralty and the most common anchor shape: an iron shank with two fluked arms.

FORE OR FORWARD: TOWARD the bow.

GAFF: A POLE with a sharp hook.

GALLEY: A BOAT'S KITCHEN and living quarters.

GREEN-TO-GREEN: PASSAGE OF TWO sea-going vessels moving in opposite directions on their starboard (right) sides.

GUNWALE: (PRONOUNCED *GUNNEL*.) The outer railing or upper edge of a hull.

HATCH: AN OPENING in the deck of a boat.

HELM: THE OPERATING components of a boat: wheel, gauges, throttle, etc.

HOQUIAM: (*Ho-kwim*) LOCAL NATIVE AMERICAN word meaning *hungry for wood*; a lumber town in western Washington; one of the five rivers that flow into Grays Harbor Bay.

HULL: WATERTIGHT lower portion of a boat.

HUMPTULIPS: (*Hum-tu-lups*) LOCAL NATIVE AMERICAN term meaning *hard to pole or chilly region;* a region in Western Washington; one of the five rivers that flow into Grays Harbor Bay.

KNOT: SPEED of one nautical mile per hour.

LAZARET: A STORAGE area on a boat.

LINES: ROPES of a boat.

LOG: A NAVIGATIONAL journal.

MAKAH: AN INDIGENOUS PEOPLE who have inhabited the northwest tip of Washington State for centuries.

MAST: A VERTICAL pole on which sails are attached.

NOR'WESTER: A FRESH WIND from the northwest

OFFSHORE: AWAY FROM shore toward deep water.

PILOTHOUSE: A GLASS-ENCLOSED room from which a boat is controlled, usually U-shaped.

PORTSIDE: The LEFT-HAND side of a boat.

PORTHOLE: A SMALL round window in a boat.

RED-TO-RED: PASSAGE OF TWO sea-going vessels moving in opposite directions on their portside (left) side.

RUDDER: A VERTICAL BLADE at the stern of a vessel that can be turned by the wheel to change direction when in motion.

SHIP THE OARS: PULLING THE OARS OUT of the water to stop rowing.

SLOUGH: SWAMPY AREA of water connected to a larger body of water.

SNOLLYGOSTER: SHREWD, unprincipled person.

SOU'WESTER: A FRESH WIND from the southwest.

SPRAY: FLYING water.

STARBOARD: The RIGHT-HAND side of a boat.

STEAM DONKEY: A Steam-powered winch.

STEM: THE BOW'S forward tip.

STERN: The back END OF A BOAT.

TAFFRAIL: The rail at the stern.

TATTING: A process where handmade lace is formed by looping and knotting a single thread with the use of a small hand shuttle and fingers.

THWART: A crosspiece spanning across the gunwales used as a seat in a rowboat.   .

THROTTLE DOWN/BACK: Reduce speed.

THROTTLE UP/OPEN: Increase speed.

TIN SHOP: An establishment where tinware is sold or made: pots, pans, plates, cups, cans, buckets, plus other items.

TRIPLE-EXPANSION: A compound steam Engine that operates three cylinders at different pressure levels.

WAKE: Turbulence behind a vessel.

WEIGH ANCHOR: To pull up the anchor from the sea floor.

WINCH: A mechanical device that with the aid of pulleys, cables, and a spool, used to hoist or release heavy loads.

ABOUT THE AUTHOR

KB Taylor's Grays Harbor family history spans back to the 1860s. The author worked as a project-control manager for an aerospace contractor in San Diego. She now resides with her husband in Washington State.

She is an award winning author of *The Seagirls of the Irene* (WILLA Literary Award, Children's Fiction) and *Hattie's Family: Through the Eyes of a Dairymaid* (WILL ROGERS Gold Medallion Award, Western Romance).

If you would like to leave a review on your favorite website, it would be much appreciated. Thanks for reading. Please visit at www.kb-taylor.com.

Made in the USA
Middletown, DE
30 March 2022